WAR IN PIECES 1
Ivan the Terrible
from Tulsa

This book is dedicated in loving memory
to four artistic mentors whom we lost in 2014.
From different perspectives, they steered my
artistic projects.

Connecticut architect Donald Baerman

New York publisher Colin Jones

Oxford historian Piers Mackesy

Manchester musician Joyce Lindley Parker

WAR IN PIECES 1
Ivan the Terrible
from Tulsa

Sean Dennis Cashman

First published in the United Kingdom in 2015
by Sixth Avenue Books

ISBN 978-0-9571281-1-8

Produced by
The Choir Press, Gloucester

Contents

TWIN TOWERS

The best of times was about to become the worst of times.

New Yorkers expected snow that February morning in 1993: not a blizzard, but flurries dusting Manhattan, picturesque before traffic turned the white film to grungy gray. But what they got Downtown was all-powerful fire.

Down into the bowels under the Twin Towers of the World Trade Center glided an unremarkable yellow Ford Econoline truck hired from Ryder. Inside, extremist Ramzi Yousef, a lean stringy man with a face like a horse, was about to detonate a massive bomb, weighing 1,200 pounds and nestling among several weighty tanks of hydrogen.

Yousef wanted to topple the Twin Towers. His plan was that the explosion would make one crash into the other, bring both down, and cause havoc across the city. Inside the van he lit four twenty-foot-long fuses. Then he dashed into a red getaway Chevrolet. He was stalled for minutes because some unexpected truck was blocking the exit. Would he be killed alongside his victims?

The van ahead moved, the path was clear, and he was on his way out.

In a split second the blast wave roared. It bellowed upwards through five resistant concrete floors. The all-powerful detonation dislodged a twelve-foot-long crossways support that weighed 14,000 pounds. In the basement a concrete wall separated a workers' lunchroom from the ramp to the public car park where the Ryder truck exploded. The blast sent the mighty crossways support shooting through the basement where workers were eating lunch. Six died instantly. Most grotesque was the death of one carrying her unborn baby.

The twin towers were plunged into darkness.

A trader on the 96th floor said, "It's just lightning."

"Lightning? In winter? When we've just had snow?"

"Wait," said another trader, holding his cell phone. "This broker says there's smoke coming out of the building. It must be an explosion inside. We'd better get out while we can."

Lower down the towers, people were jolted from their office tasks as the entire building shook. Overhead lights flashed off and on. Computers went down. Almost immediately, people were surrounded by swirling smoke. Many thought they were facing sudden death. Panic spread down the floors as workers headed for the nearest stairwells.

However, the stairwells were pitch black. Hardly anyone had torches. The people behind were pressing hard on those in front. It was as if they were kicking their way downstairs. It seemed that people lower down might be crushed by this mighty tsunami of humanity—a fumbling human chain in the stairwell. It was getting hotter with each step.

"Suppose we meet a wall of flame?" whispered one woman.

"It's like *Towering Inferno*."

"Don't imagine. Just keep moving."

By the time they reached the 60th floor, they were in a hot panic.

Somehow they managed to get a second wind.

As they reached floors in the twenties, the end of their ordeal was—just possibly—in sight. The human centipede turned an emotional corner and quickened its pace. It was no longer a slow-moving marathon but a race, a dash to the finish: open door and light.

Breathless, panting, and wheezing, people tumbled out, some falling on others. Those others were hacking up blood. They were drenched in sweat and sapped of energy. The smoky atmosphere outside seemed sweeter by far than the foul odor of the acrid stairwells. Gray was the sky and white were their faces but that was underneath the dark stain of soot that covered them. Later, they might recall the dark stain as a badge of courage, for they were New Yorkers.

For years to come the center of this terrifying blast would be known across the globe as Ground Zero.

Disaster was a great leveler among survivors outside. Throngs of fire fighters, police officers, and paramedics who had come to aid the victims of the explosion saw no visible signs to distinguish the staggering wounded. Their faces were blackened—stained by soot and filth from the explosion. They belched the debris onto the slush and snow. It was like a massacre of the innocents, a snow scene polluted by murder. But there was, as yet, no one to blame for the tragedy.

Handsome Turk Darius Esen was on his way to meet secret girlfriend Holly Wood when the explosion seemed to rock the ground under him. He did not know exactly what had happened but his guess was accurate enough. He felt he had been drawn into a vortex of escalating fanaticism guilty step by guilty step in New Jersey. And now the terrorists had exploded their bomb.

From his safe distance, he thought of the deep panic within the innocent people in the towers. It seemed some were plucking up courage, debating whether to jump out of the windows, weighing up whether to plunge helter-skelter to their deaths, or die, crushed within the towers if they crumbled. Darius was too much of a coward to do anything that might betray him. It had taken this disaster—which he should never have been part of, no matter how remote—for him to realize how much Holly meant to him. Now she was lost to him forever.

Holly was coming back from the funeral of her manager, Brad Gable, in Jersey City. Rather than use a glossy university car, which would have been conspicuous, she chose public transport in order to stay anonymous. She had deliberately selected her least stylish clothes. She had traveled early from New England by Metro North to Manhattan, taken the subway downtown and then the PATH train under the Hudson so that she could sidle unremarked into the modest church outside Jersey City.

She had felt nothing during the service, not even residual anger for Brad's cruel jibe in the jazz club a few years ago. When it was over in the graveyard, she hailed a taxi for the PATH train station in Jersey City. She was not going to her friends' planned intervention with her loathsome husband in the restaurant. She was going to escape. Within her dreary outfit, Holly was burning with feverish anticipation. It was not just that escape from her terrible marriage was imminent—it was her yearning for Darius's way of making love.

The return journey through New Jersey was the same: a raggle-taggle mix of buildings on downtown strips and dreary stations until she reached the gloomy tiles, dull walls, and drab atmosphere of the PATH station below the World Trade Center. But, as she started to make her way out of the PATH station, there was an almighty crash. Jolted, Holly did not know what to make of the bang and the rumble. Everything seemed to be tumbling. She did not know if it was walls or ceilings but she recognized pipes. It was as if she had entered a 3-D version of one of her husband's prized paintings of mangled bodies in World War II.

There was a man aside the track partly covered with rubble. He was calling out in agony. When she bent down, she saw something sticking out of his back. She could hardly believe that in this disaster—whatever it was— someone would knife him for his wallet. Then she realized that it was inches of bone coming out of his back.

"Stay quiet," she said as she knelt beside him. "We'll get help."

4

Only after Holly had spoken did she realize that she had said this. A little later, she knew she had taken off her coat and placed it over him without recalling having done this either. She folded her scarf and placed it under his head.

The noise was deafening. It was a horror movie all right. A man, crumpled aside the victim she was trying to tend to, had his clothes off. His flesh was flaking from his upper body and fluttering in the swirling smoke.

Terrorist Ramzi Yousef was already at his getaway vantage point in New Jersey. Within minutes of the explosion, he watched the catastrophe from the shoreline. He was expecting, hoping, to see first one tower collapse in voluminous clouds of debris, smoke, and pulverized humanity and then the other tower tumble alongside. Did the towers sway like palms shifted by a mighty hurricane? Surely, inside, it must seem that they shook.

But the towers were still there. Was there time to curse that the explosion had not gone according to plan? No, he had to make good his escape via a genie in the sky flying across the oceans. That very day he flew to Karachi in Pakistan using his real name: Abdul Basit Karim.

A few clients were settling down for lunch at the Golden Cockerel, a restaurant on East 50th Street, when the news came through. Imelda, the Filipino chef, heard it first on Ten Ten Wins radio in the kitchen upstairs. She practically tumbled downstairs to the lobby, even more startling in her cross-dressing costume of red halter top and designer jeans because of her scared delivery: "They've done it. Car bomb. Lots of blood. Downtown closed."

Cesare Groznyy, president of Babel City University, realized that he was going to have to stay in the restaurant he had come to detest. He had gone there for a working lunch with a press reporter whom he planned to bribe in an attempt to disrupt the education panel's hearings against

5

him. But his various guests would not get there: transport had stalled.

Groznyy skimmed the surface of the lentil soup and picked at stray leaves in the green salad. The dark circles round his blinking eyes made him look like a frightened panda. Yet his gloom had not blunted his sense of irony. He glanced at the picture above the sepia marble fireplace, a copy of *The Three Graces* by Joshua Reynolds. They looked down contemptuously.

Then news about the bomb became more specific. The owner of the delicatessen next door came in. He explained that, minutes after midday, a Ryder truck with 1,500 pounds of explosives had detonated in the underground garage of the North Tower.

"Of course," said a Know-All diner from the United Nations, "New York has always been a focus for terrorism. From time to time terrorists have targeted famous venues to draw attention to their causes. In the 1970s the Puerto Rican independence movement exploded bombs in Manhattan. FBI officers don't like to believe the Big Apple is a Mecca for terrorists. But the long tale of attacks in the city tells its own story."

Cesare Groznyy took all this as a portent of personal disaster. He wanted light. There was a giant window of numerous small square panes in the restaurant carved out of the townhouse. The window opened onto a fringe of yard no deeper than three feet and shielded by an ugly wall of concrete blocks ten feet high. Cloudy sky peeped down from above as if it longed to cast natural light into the dining room. Artificial light came from an outsize Marie Antoinette chandelier and some tawdry wall lights with glass pendants. Tacky enough for the trustees and the reporters Groznyy wanted to bribe, but too déclassé for him.

Groznyy had never noticed the grandmother clock in the hall before. Now its penetrating ticking was irritating

6

beyond endurance, tick-tick-tocking away to his damnation. He looked up at the obese restaurateur moving towards him. Groznyy realized that here was someone who represented nemesis, the owner of this paltry restaurant, his hidey-hole for dark deeds: Benny Vincenzo.

Benny Vincenzo looked like the famous gouache of Oscar Wilde in Paris painted shortly before his death by Toulouse Lautrec: a powder-puff balloon of a man, like the prince regent stuffed to extinction. His hair was a silken cascade of gray curls adorning a balloon face in which nestled pursed lips. His eyes were almost closed by surrounding fat but wide staring with razor-sharp intelligence as he surveyed the world. He rarely traveled beyond his block and round the corner to 2nd Avenue. You could tell under his steady eyes that his sharp mind all but spat out his contempt for Groznyy. He looked at Groznyy with the disdain of a spider that had caught a trifling fly in his web but could wait to dine on his revenge when it was cold. Then he would suck out its blood.

When Benny came back into the dining room, he handed Groznyy a hastily scrawled note on a slip of pink paper. It told Groznyy his journalist guest had called to say that he might not be able to make the meeting.

Head and shoulders, Cesare Groznyy looked like the bust of a particularly dissolute emperor of ancient Rome in its decline—even down to the ashen complexion akin to bleached, worn marble. His pugilistic expression, carved out of features both podgy and brutal, taken with his twisted, blunted nose, his opulent lips turned down on one side, all suggested barely repressed anger. But this was not scorn against the world but, rather, anger bottled up against himself, his hatred of his own hollow innards.

Benny started talking. His barbs hit home.

"Your old-fashioned plays—so many begin in an inn with travelers hollering for dinner. What the plays served up in their tired old plots is the leading players—especially the heroines—to be digested by the audience, consumed—what do feminists say? —exploited—as well as by the villains."

Benny paused slightly before the word "villains."

Groznyy sensed there was some further mystery in this shabby Manhattan townhouse-turned-restaurant, a business created by the late Princess Glinskaya, whom he called aunt. He thought it should be his by rights but this accursed sodomite had somehow stolen it from him. While he picked at his filet mignon, he heard a key turn in the lock of a door cut into the wall. Instinctively, Groznyy knew he was about to experience a second coming, a resurrection. He braced himself as She in her swirling cape, turned into the dining room. Other diners saw a striking mature woman wearing a turquoise turban with iridescent gold thread and a black cape that set off a multicolored choker necklace. Her bony face took in everything with an imperious glare.

She simply said, "Zdrazvitye, little prince, tsaryevitch."

"Babulenka," stumbled out of his mouth. He had long wondered and part dreaded when it would happen—her reappearance.

"Just as you thought I was gone. Yes, how desperately you must have wanted to persuade yourself that some old woman's sodden body pulled from the East River and that you identified as me really was me."

Princess Nadezhda Arachnova Glinskaya sat on the empty chair opposite like an unwanted shadow. She thrust down a newspaper, opened at page three. Again, he guessed what was coming, a cartoon insulting him. When he saw the newspaper cartoon of himself as the Old Woman Who Lived in a Shoe playing host to all manner of naughty trustees and administrators, he steeled himself. For there it was again: the signature of his dear dead son, Modest.

"You thought Modest was gone, like me, didn't you? But his talent as an artist lives on in these cartoons, the spirit of humor."

"Still wearing a crucifix?" Groznyy asked impudently. "I suppose it contains poison, the everyday trapping of a Russian lady of quality?"

"That won't be necessary. You've had enough poison already."

She patted her peculiar choker necklace. It seemed to be made of strips of myriad-colored paper, tightly woven and glued into strings of little balls. He had seen such a necklace before but could not think where.

"Rather down-market," he said. "No diamonds or pearls?"

"It has sentimental value—gift of a dear, loyal friend. Besides, the demons boiling the brew that is your destiny are not interested in my dress sense."

Groznyy did not want to take any more but the damned bomb blast made it impossible to escape. The princess turned to Benny Vincenzo.

"It's strange for him to be so quiet. First, he ensures his personality overwhelms everyone else. Then, he expects his family and his disillusioned employees to bend the knee before him, the sovereign prize ram, turning his university into a corrupt court of lickspittle toads. He's sick, psychologically sick. Didn't you know that, caro Benny?

Cesare sensed blood rising in his sallow cheeks.

"And the upshot?" She reeled off a prepared list: "Two universities, two murders, two suicides, one fire, one death by exposure. Quite a tally for little Ivan the Terrible. And the personal climax? Two career deaths, one past, one imminent. And the best joke is: our modern Ivan the Terrible has become Ivan the Terrified."

Groznyy was getting beside himself. She was enjoying it.

"Well, as you reflect, what was your worst mistake? Let's put it this way: when Ivan the Terrible takes on Holly Wood, he loses everything."

Groznyy exploded. Down came the table, with its cutlery and crockery. Since the table was just a frame of worn legs

9

with a round top ledged upon it covered with a simple white cloth, down came food and drink. Everything was crumpled together on the stained cloth as Groznyy tried to swat the damn princess. She fell back on top of the buffoon restaurateur at the precise moment when two photographers burst in with their white flashes and shoulder-held TV cameras capturing it all.

Out of nowhere came Groznyy's two Mafioso-style counselors, Larry Dawdler and Bogus Revisor—surprised like the other players.

As waiters scurried to put things right, Benny apologized to the few remaining diners.

"No need, Benny," said a Rockefeller. "We got our money's worth with this psychological cabaret."

Fifteen minutes later, outside the shabby townhouse that housed the Golden Cockerel, Princess Glinskaya faced a small TV crew being ordered about by chic blonde New Yorker Kelly Danson. With a rising red weal across her wizened cheek, the ancient princess delivered her rehearsed speech.

"If you ask Cesare Groznyy about his personal history, you will get a series of half truths of a heroic past. They are the clue to him and his path of destruction at Babel City University."

"How did Groznyy come to America?" Kelly asked the princess.

"The upheaval of World War II—what Russians call the Second Great Patriotic War—allowed him to escape to Western Europe. He supported partisans against the Germans, facing down invading soldiers with machine guns. He's still facing down—or so he thinks—enemies but with his rhetoric, that's his new weapon of choice."

The princess was satisfied with her performance. But she was furious with everyone else. When the reporters left, she exploded to Benny.

"How dare they bomb the World Trade Center and upstage me? We were all prepared—apart from Holly—where the hell was she? But to find we will be buried in today's TV news and tomorrow's papers! Damn them to hell!"

Later, in her seashore home, Holly had never felt so alone. "What a fool I've been," she said. "Color him gone."

Survivors and emergency heroes thought long and hard about the reasons for the 1993 attack on the twin towers. What would they do?

1980s

THE NEW CAESAR

"Nemo? Nemo? You can't possibly be 'Nemo'—'nobody'—and you certainly can't stay 'Nemo.'"

His mentor was speaking. Groznyy listened. Together they were surveying the panorama of the twin cities of Norse Hoven and Babel City from the Crown Tower of Milhous College aside Norse Hoven Green.

It was one of the first couronne, or crown, towers in Gothic style built for hundreds of years. It had been constructed as a memorial to Milhous College students killed in World War I. And its pealing carillon was played twice a day to remind people. The tower was decorated with gargoyles of abstract virtues and fanciful college stereotypes.

Enraptured by the illogical mix of towers and turrets that was the roof-scape of Milhous College, Groznyy paused before answering. He was mesmerized by the decorative masonry with its sculpted coils of cord, its lions and dragons, its balconies and gargoyles.

"My parents named me 'Nemo' because they wanted a neutral name, not Russian, not Slav, not Tartar. 'Nemo' was to show I owed allegiance to no group. They hoped I might escape the Soviet Union and Stalin's terrors."

"That you might rise from nowhere to become somebody—you—a Russian born outside Russia, in Venice?"

"That's one story."

"Or Tulsa?"

"That's another."

Groznyy knew better than to give anything away to

Franklin Miller, the snowy-haired academic with penetrating blue eyes, corduroy clothes, and a walking cane. Miller's benign manner did not cover his ruthless political skill and adroit self-promotion. These he had learned as a CIA operative. Rumor with many tongues had it that if, and when, the right sort of Republican president came to power, then Miller would be in line for ambassador to some Far East country. He had once worked there on the extraordinary rendition of partisans opposed to US foreign policy, spiriting them away for confessions obtained by extraordinary means.

Miller continued his verbal assault: "Then, there's Groznyy: 'Terrible.'"

"'Awesome,' that's what our Russian word means."

"But it's better understood as 'Terrible.' In the West we don't say 'Ivan Groznyy,' we say 'Ivan the Terrible'. Well, Nemo the Awesome, your parents would never live to see your escape."

He had watched Nemo Groznyy progress from eager graduate student to ambitious assistant professor at NYU, New York University; Miller thought he had never seen so intense or so charismatic a face.

"Looking over this panorama, it's like Toledo in Spain, isn't it or, maybe, Florence from the hills? A bleached city of houses, factories—everything gleaming in the morning sun. What do you see?"

"Farms. A marina with little boats. A fair—or maybe it's a circus."

Nemo felt he was back in grad school. Miller had taught him advocacy—how to get an argument across.

"What does all this below us suggest to you, you with the ability to bring out subtext in every statement?"

"A circus suggests the makeshift nature of human lives as well as a womb. A farm symbolizes fertility. A ship moored in the harbor suggests the waves of destiny that carry the human race forward."

Franklin Miller smiled. This is just what he wanted. With Nemo Groznyy, all was surface verbal dexterity so as to imply uncommon insights and unifying themes. Wonderful for the front man he intended Groznyy to be. Even his voice was perfect for he spoke English with neither an English nor an American accent but with what Miller called an Omar Sharif voice: a charming, indeterminate accent with seductive tones. That must be his secret with women, not his bedroom eyes, certainly not his spindly frame. No wonder he was already on to his second wife. Or was it his third? And young Groznyy also had the brute instincts of a street fighter.

Nemo was beginning to guess that they were going to move here.

"Do you see anything else?"

"Spires, towers. Around us buildings of the great Milhous College; farther away little Norse Hoven University and the bigger Babel City University. Two cities: three universities."

"Let's move from long shot to close up."

Miller had also been staring at the crown tower's decorations, its allegorical gargoyles representing such abstract concepts as War and Peace, Truth and Justice, and Progress and Freedom. They made him uneasy. It was obvious that Groznyy hankered after a place in the sun there. And Miller could tell that he was thinking wistfully about the gargoyles representing Ivy League life—a scholar, an athlete, and a tea-drinking socialite.

They drove to Babel City University. The contrast with Milhous College was depressing. There was no classical facade with cool portico, no Gothic front with arches for this university. They stopped at the modern student center with its giant hall that could be subdivided by cascading partition walls—just like any conference hotel. The canteen had slot machines with fizzy drinks, chocolate bars, and automat entrees.

14

Nemo started to wax lyrical over every fault.

"The facade is faux Scandinavian. It has soaring triangular shapes, some pushing out diagonally so that everything but the main auditorium—which has to be functional—is ill-shaped with corners too awkward to clean. It needs renovation and this is a college with next to no funds."

"Yes," said Franklin Miller. He waited.

"You're leaving New York; you're coming here as provost, or whatever they call the chief academic officer?"

"I'm coming as president."

"And you want me to come as a professor?"

"I want you to come here as provost—to come the year after me."

Nemo knew he was under-qualified. But Miller was in full flow.

"We need to make Babel City University, with its impoverished minds, a first-class college. As president, I will raise the money. Much of the infrastructure—physical plant, research labs, and personnel—is in place. I want you to be my bruiser—to make sure we raise the academic profile of the professors."

"So that was it," thought Nemo. "He is asking me to make a pact with him. I get position in exchange for becoming an enforcer. I'll be damned if I'll do his bidding without getting my reward on my terms."

Miller read Nemo's mind and was enjoying the psychological torture.

"You think of devils as Machiavellian figures, sinister manipulators with devastating irony: Mephistopheles in *Faust*, Iago in *Othello*. These devils tempt devout people, offering to fulfill their secret desires in exchange for their souls."

"He'll never have my soul," thought Nemo.

"The modern version of this in pulp fiction is the multinational company that gives the earth to ambitious

15

newcomers in business, or the law, or politics—marvelous salaries, lavish lifestyles. But what they are doing is making them dependent, and sucking the life out of them."

They were back to basics.

"As I said, you can't remain 'Nemo'—'no one'—too German—'Nehemiah'—too Jewish. You need a name that complements Groznyy: Caesar. Cesare Groznyy—that's better. And it has the connotation of 'czar.'"

Thus it was, with nothing beside his charisma, that Nemo Groznyy, a little red devil, found himself the new Cesare Groznyy and the new provost at Babel City University in New England.

President Franklin Miller's initial reputation as a successful college president at BCU came from his fiscal reforms and modernizing administration. The professors basked in a glow of expectation. They enjoyed idealized projections and a surfeit of lavish entertainment. Now came the reality of reform. Miller introduced his new provost.

While Miller planned to reinvent academia in New England, Groznyy's elderly relative was reinventing dining out in New York. She was interviewing the perfect candidate for manager.

"I wanted to create a restaurant that made everyone feel as comfortable as if they were in their own home—except that everything was perfection."

Princess Nadezhda Glinskaya was aglow with self-admiration.

"The restaurant is my folly. Even if Cesare Groznyy helped fund it, it's mine not his. He has his little fiefdom in little BCU. I have mine."

Before her Benny Vincenzo cut a stately figure. The princess could tell he would run to fat, but she liked that because she thought it would give her clientele an impression of opulence. She scrutinized his face. She could tell it was losing its original fine-drawn features. Nevertheless, it remained expressive. Sometimes, it would change as if fired up inside by some Italian devil's eyes—eyes that never flickered. Their irises were steadfast and the eyelids open so as to frame the staring expression. He was perfect, first as her manager, a little later, as her heir.

Benny was appraising her creation.

Originally a shabby townhouse with four stories on a street in Manhattan's East Fifties, it housed two dark apartments on the upper floors, one for him, one for her.

Along the winding corridor was the main dining area in an extension to the original townhouse. It had been constructed on the house garden. It extended two stories high. Inside, the restaurant reached upwards to the second floor of the house. There was an aperture onto the back wall from its Juliet balcony, creating a musicians' gallery whence flowed pianissimo muzak.

To compensate for the loss of a real garden, the princess had created an ersatz inner garden on the inside. It was in a modest alcove room separated from the main restaurant by two sets of French doors. This alcove sheltered a make-believe Italian garden such as you might find in a Roman palazzo. It had a tiny, sparkling fountain, two stone cherubs, one plastic angel, and a profusion of Mediterranean flowers: bougainvillea, mimosa, and acacia.

"Everything is artificial with all the exquisite delicacy of synthetic flowers that no country can perfect as well as the United States," murmured the princess.

Indeed, Benny could see how this cherished rookery garden nook enhanced the Golden Cockerel's secluded character. As a diner, once you entered and moved along the corridor, you entered a discrete world as different from the high-energy atmosphere of Midtown as countryside or seashore.

The midst of the dining area immediately under the huge

central chandelier hosted a round service table with cutlery, plates, glasses, and bottles of red wine. An outsize bouquet of artificial red roses surmounted it.

"Who do you think are my clients?"

Benny paused.

"Your clientele is wide-ranging. It's led by United Nations diplomats and by what remains of New York robber-baron families. There are also executives from Corporate America and clerical staff from Midtown."

"Let's talk turkey," said the princess with another abrupt change of tone. She handed Benny a flier.

"To make things easier for everyone—you, me, and the customers—here is the typical menu of our atypical restaurant. Everything is included in the *prix fixe*—your lunch at $35, your dinner at $45. Each sitting has five courses and as much red or white wine as you care for. If you want hard liquor, it comes neat or on the rocks, or in a cocktail, costing a uniform $6. Can you make a whiskey sour? On the rocks?"

After fumbling in the foyer bar, Benny handed her the cocktail. All the princess said as she sipped it was, "I prefer mine made so strong as to knock you up sharp."

Benny's curiosity got the better of him.

"Your great nephew helped you open the restaurant? He's a sleeping partner?"

"You could say that. All he wants in return is use of a special room."

The princess led the way, mounting the stairs unsteadily to the second floor. There she opened a room opposite the kitchen, one that faced south onto the tree-lined street. It was a comfortable-sized room for a private party that could accommodate a dozen or so people around a lengthy table. The walls had a faded emerald-green wallpaper and carried reproductions of lithographs of old London: St Paul's Cathedral with its great dome peeping above the hurly burly of Fleet Street during a 1920s rush hour.

18

"They wouldn't be out of place in a college alumnus club on Vanderbilt Avenue beside Grand Central Station," observed Benny.

The princess gave him an unforgiving look.

Benny said, "So, that's the point. Art wrapping up the past as a calming reflection of assurance. Not New York but old London. Where the main restaurant is Mediterranean rococo escapism, upstairs we emphasize the solidity of banking. But a foggy London, nevertheless—murky for murky deeds, suggesting integrity is a facade."

"I couldn't possibly comment," said the princess, repeating a line from a British TV import on *Masterpiece Theatre*. "Let's go downstairs."

They sat in the tiny front bar. Benny took up the one-page menu, left on fliers at the front door, along with souvenir white marbles with the restaurant's logo: a cockerel crowing. As he started reading the menu, she took it from him and said with smiling insistence, "But it is part of your job description to advise guests what to select."

"I'll need to familiarize myself with the choices."

"There's no time like the present. It's a quarter of twelve. The first guests will arrive in fifteen minutes."

As he took orders, Benny oiled his way from table to table with what would become his customary introduction, "We have some nice items today."

Streamlined efficiency was how Benny managed the restaurant for his first months. He worked out which waiters could do the job honestly and which waiters could not. Sensing that Bernardo was the most pliant, he persuaded the princess to reselect staff from Bernardo's own Dominican family—brothers, cousins, and nephews. The princess was amazed at Benny's efficiency: "It's more than your training at catering school. You're a natural. Everything is choreographed. Now we can discuss our futures, yours and mine."

*

Cesare Groznyy, new provost of Babel City University, planned to have them eating out of his hands that Halloween night. All of them: professors, students, and families. All were to be mesmerized by his first speech.

You could have heard a pin drop when he mounted the podium in the auditorium with its partition walls folded aside to accommodate everyone. The expectant audience saw a middle-aged man of medium height, tubby and bow-legged. Whether attired for work or leisure, by now they knew Groznyy was always immaculately coutured. The dark navy-blue suits with a soupcon of gray pin stripe and the starched pin-stripe blue shirts adorned with blazing-colored ties were intended as the dress-to-kill display of a first-class mind soaring above minnows in the dank pond of university politics. Unfortunately, when he skittered up the steps and across the platform, the way Groznyy's trousers flapped at half-mast above his ankles undermined his presumption of superiority. He scowled.

"Is modern man in charge of his own destiny or is he following the herd? That is the question before us at Babel City University. It is time for us to wake up—not to continue like babes sleeping because they are lost in a wood.

"Asleep? Perrault's legend of Sleeping Beauty awaiting true love in an enchanted place inspired Tchaikovsky in a ballet that made her immortal. That old bore, Wagner, gave her a stirring battle cry in opera. But while Brunnhilde, the fat lady, our Sleeping Beauty, our little BCU, is still asleep, the world around her is changing."

From the front row, a little lady with white wispy hair in an untidy chignon and a striking choker necklace observed in a southern accent, "Talks kinda purdy, don't he?"

"He speaks preposterous English. It's like a flotilla of decaying sponges," whispered her son beside her.

"Babel City University has long served as a junior college, providing a base from which to launch careers at

Ivy League schools, and even Oxford, Cambridge, and the Sorbonne.

"However, the recent economic downturn has brought BCU's underlying financial difficulties to a head. Such a crisis of capitalism! Something you tender Marxists have long predicted. How ironic you are no longer in a position to turn it to your advantage!"

Groznyy knew without looking that this salvo would hit the mark, as his old street trader adversary from their student days, Mordred Stickleman, was now in the audience as an associate professor of economic history.

"Dearest friends, we have to accept that our local student base is dwindling because of adverse demographic factors—an aging population and declining numbers of young people. Now little Babel City University must look outside its immediate geographic area for students. We must improve our academic programs.

"Do not despair: I am here. Babel City University may be broke but it is not poor. Many societies have faced comparable dilemmas. Previous civilizations have had to surmount them. Let's go back five hundred years.

"Immortality is the future prize of prophets. The great scientist Galileo understood this with his discovery that the Earth revolved around the Sun. The implications of Galileo's revelation went wider than astronomy and physics. This was a trumpet call to arms. The church said the Earth was flat. The topsy-turvy political implications of Galileo's findings spelled revolution to the church and the established political order.

"What has this got to do with our dwindling fortunes? Every work force has its careerists: established men—and women—with families. If family men—and women—rock the boat of conventional wisdom, they may put their families at risk. Who is the true careerist? The man who obeys conventional wisdom and keeps his job? Or the man who seeks truth, may lose his job, but keeps his immortal soul?"

"Groznyy has stolen all this from Michelangelo," said Ace Ferrari, dean of psychology. Then he added, "And Shostakovich."

Groznyy was in full flight.

"To return to Galileo, the man who moved heaven and earth: political pressure and the threat of torture frightened him into recanting. What does that tell us? Present success depends on conformity. But our future depends on progressive thinking. That is uncomfortable. But that is what I ask all of us at BCU to do, not simply to thrive but to survive. Don't be afraid. We are all traveling to the same destination: academic excellence."

When Groznyy finished, he smacked his lips as if he was flourishing a trumpet. Then he was no longer relaxed, no longer a rider but, instead, a hound trying to find his prey. Groznyy knew the applause was hollow.

"The ego has landed," said the dean of psychology.

Stickleman answered, "Yup, the Bionic Mouth of Ivan the Terrible."

The tired little English professor escorted his white-haired mother away, telling her, "As a devil, he's more than plausible—he's a genius of manipulation—narrative, plot, and people."

His mother did not understand her son's words but she soon would.

Groznyy still felt the chill of audience resentment. Aloud, he heard himself say, "Everyone—students and professors, parents and neighbors—please come to our reception as honored guests."

As he walked to the reception in another building, the new provost eyed the president's house farther down the street with ill-concealed jealousy. Designed by Richard Morris Hunt, doyen of classic architects in the 1880s, it was inspired by palazzos of the Italian Renaissance. President Franklin Miller had already set about restoring its precious murals and vaulted ceilings.

Groznyy had a taste for the high life. He had already noticed two blocks over in Milhous Avenue another handsome mansion that had grown from its nineteenth-century origins, having been extended with turrets and oriel windows. It looked like a Gothic fantasy, isolated and forlorn, as might have been painted by Edward Hopper or filmed by Alfred Hitchcock.

Groznyy coveted it and had already made enquiries. It seemed that the house had belonged to a distinguished scientist of Babel City University, recently deceased. When he died, he bequeathed it jointly to his daughter from his first marriage, to his second wife, and to her son by her own first marriage. The daughter lived with her own family three towns over. The scientist's widow, Beth Helene, and her son, Ashley Bedfellow Burns, professor of southern literature at BCU, still lived in the house.

Groznyy was mulling over how he could acquire the house for the university and then have it assigned to him. He was also planning a cull of professors. The second problem provided the solution to the first. His tool and victim was Ashley Bedfellow Burns. Personally unknown to him, the first two victims of Ivan the Terrible from Tulsa arrived at the reception: the generous, naive mother and her disappointed son. They were lambs to the slaughter.

Ashley felt unsure of his small size, his receding chin, his poor eyesight, and his lack of sex appeal. His family had come from Alsace—although how the original French "Belle Fleuve" had become the English "Bedfellow," no one knew. Ashley's mother, Beth, had a whiff of Parisian charm that decorated her cornpone manner.

Beth's mind was set in the worn living room of her New

England home just as it had been in the 1940s with its handsome, worn staircases and threadbare furnishings. Everything spoke of parochial values awaiting further electric-shock treatment from TV, cars, and recorded sound—the very things that had made American culture roar in the American century.

As a child, Ashley had been serious with a decided academic bent. His defense mechanism against neighbors who thought him mighty strange was a waspish wit. He always had a lingering doubt that the root cause of his failure was never having been in the right place at the right time. If there had been an "Armies of the Night" march on the Pentagon in protest at American involvement in Vietnam when he was a grad student, he had stayed away. Yet he had marveled at the supreme self-sacrifice of Buddhist monks by immolation during the war in Vietnam.

At one of his lectures at BCU he had faced a sea of indifferent faces. When he took off his eyeglasses—the better to scrutinize his notes—the ample hairstyles of maids before him seemed like outrageous birds' nests.

"Shakespeare's play, *Richard III*, was the last of his four plays in sequence—about dynastic warfare among the English nobility. It took place during the Hundred Years War between England and France. Shakespeare had told both stories simultaneously in his preceding *Henry VI* plays."

Ashley decided to cultivate the feminist vote.

"Who was the French warrior heroine from Lorraine whose exploits kick-started the French campaign to oust the English from France?"

Silence.

"She was only seventeen when she started."

Ashley decided to break the silence with another clue.

"She was only nineteen when she fell, captured by the English. She met the same fate as our own dear White

House from the English attack in 1812: elimination by burning. Who was she? What was she called?"

More silence.

Then, to his relief, a timid person with her hair in plaits raised her hand. He nodded expectantly.

"Could it be?" asked the timorous voice: "Madame Curie?"

Ashley was more nonplussed than any student. Chemist Madame Curie? Surely, she was half Polish? Surely she arrived on the scene four-and-a-half centuries after Joan of Arc? The student might just as well have said "Marie Antoinette."

Joan of Arc may have died a human fireball but Ashley Bedfellow Burns knew his rocket had fallen to earth like the dry stick he had become.

What the students saw was a shriveled soul. As Ashley fumbled through his class, he stumbled figuratively over the girls' décolleté blouses. While he yearned for the girls, pretty or plain, they found him repulsive. He would invite a senior or a grad student out for a drink. But heavy breathing never graduated to petting. He tried to date Hermione Eterna, a young Milhous student taking some summer classes at BCU. She had a budding Titianesque figure. She was nervous in the bar and it showed as she kept touching her luxurious hair in time to when he kept touching his earlobe.

Feeling alienated from professors and students, Ashley took his case to various bars. He was never sober. He drank for breakfast, lunch, and dinner. Nor was he a happy or a silent drunk.

The legend of his Joan of Arc fiasco spread across campus. Now it became a centerpiece of conversation at the reception given by the provost.

It was supposed to be a glittering occasion. The Colonial chandeliers twinkled, the wine glasses clinked at the toast to the university, and professors who had skimped on dinner devoured the canapés like piglets at a trough.

Conversations at the reception sputtered over pleasantries but burst into heart-warming flames when lit up by tasty scandals. Professors duly prevailed upon Ashley to retell his story of student incompetence to people who had forgotten their own youthful shortcomings. When it came to the punch line about Madame Curie, everyone felt the provost's dark eyes were reappraising them.

"Hey, you, Mr. Professor, why, with all her credentials as a new thinker—challenging men in their medieval forte—has Joan of Arc not become an icon of the feminist movement?"

Ashley was nonplussed.

"Surely you had the opportunity to wax lyrical on the prequel origins of feminism, about how Joan of Arc was my hero, your hero, the feminists' hero, my grandmother's hero, in fact, everyone's hero?"

Sullen silence.

At the rear of the little group stood Mordred Stickleman. He was a tall, spindly man with a pockmarked face partly hidden by his good head of wiry gray hair. Having spiked Ashley's drink, Stickleman was in his element when it came to stories of student inadequacy as he swung his bottle of Heineken to and fro. He had a corking tale to tell.

"After I outlined various possibilities for our war with Spain in 1898, I simply asked, 'So, why did America go to war with Spain in 1898?' There was no response. Nothing came back about a conflict of commercial imperialism, the political and religious affinities of the Filipinos, or human-rights abuses in Cuba. There was nothing about the pulp fictions of the rival yellow-press syndicates.

"But, unlike poor Ashley's case, there was not deathly silence either. The lovely young nurse practitioner in the front row brimmed with confidence as she raised her arm aloft with an all-purpose American answer.

"'Why did the United States go to war in 1898?' she repeated. 'Why, to stop the spread of communism.'

"There was no reckoning that 1898 was almost twenty years before the Russian Revolution of 1917."

Again the super-intelligent mind of the provost was ahead of them.

"You could have made more of subtext. It was the all-purpose application of dogma underlying Corporate America's stance in the Cold War, the McCarthy witch hunts, the Korean War, Vietnam, and the current US drive to down the USSR: To Stop the Spread of Communism."

"It certainly did that all right," remarked the dean of psychology. "Here it is again, the long conflict between the United States and Communist Russia, two philosophies, two economies. On one side, democratic capitalism and the Fourteen Points. On the other, all-pervasive Socialism through the dictatorship of the proletariat—the age-old tale of Russian dictatorships from Ivan the Terrible to Joseph Stalin and beyond.

"And when there's a conflict between the US and the Soviet Union, it's always Hollywood that wins."

This was enough to let the little group disperse.

Ace Ferrari stood aside to let Groznyy pass. He was a good-looking man who commanded respect because of his courteous manner. Conscious that his Middle Eastern origins made him a perpetual outsider, he was able to trade on the generosity of the American people. He used his culti-vated charm to worm his way into the affections of everyone. Thus he had risen to become dean of psychology. This was easy because he was a playing a part.

Ferrari was always beautifully turned out. He wore immaculate suits cut to enhance his handsome figure. And he changed his style of clothes successively to whatever was new masculine fashion, whether it was jacket length to show the natural cut of a tight butt or sleeve length to show more cuff just like Cary Grant. That was the way Ferrari chose to blend in, although he was always a cut above any of his peers.

No one really knew his origins. Was he Palestinian or Pakistani, Afghani or Saudi Arabian? All they could be sure of was that he was a skilled academic psychologist. Indeed, he was biding his time at BCU, ready for a far-reaching purpose. He did not want Groznyy spoiling things.

"What on earth have you done?" Ferrari asked Franklin Miller seeing that the president had returned from Vienna.

"What have I done?"

"Appointing this man who thinks he has the genius of Galileo and that he, too, can move heaven and earth at 'little BCU.'"

"What have I done?" answered the president, giving nothing away.

"Cesare Groznyy, Nemo Groznyy—or whoever he is— enjoys his narcissistic character disorder. But it's us, your employees, who will have to suffer. He expects everything to flow from him, the prize ram. He will turn university governance into a corrupt court of abject toads."

"The dean is right," said Stickleman who had sidled into the conversation. "This guy has serious psychological problems. He's obsessed with his image. His self-importance has obliterated any sense of perspective. Besides, he's way too impulsive."

"Impulsive?" asked the president.

"What about his rages? He's mentally disturbed," said the dean.

Groznyy was back among them. Everyone sensed that some psychological explosion was imminent. The crowd dispersed and the storm cloud evaporated.

Next morning the provost's secretary, Bee Flute, found a surprise gathering of students at her office door. This line of twenty or so students astonished even the provost. Their leader handed him a hastily typed petition, calling for the removal of English professor Ashley Bedfellow Burns. The petition said he was a lush who had not graded a single paper that semester.

The self-appointed leader of the little delegation was an assertive girl with unruly hair. She said her name was Dolly Drum and that she came from Long Island—hence her floppy blouse in a startling floral print.

"He comes in, smelling of booze, red in the face, splutters his way through class with tales of his Georgian grandmother and we learn nothing. There are twenty-five students in the class. Not one of us has had our first paper back with grades and comments."

The provost, whose idea of effective authority was that professors should be so terrified in his presence that they wanted to shrink their asses and void their bowels, was incandescent on the students' behalf. Yet he had the greatest difficulty in trying to propitiate the students while simultaneously venting his wrath on the accused Bedfellow Burns with the promise that "Something Will Be Done."

The provost summoned the chair of the English Department who admitted that Ashley Bedfellow Burns was becoming a serious problem, what with his drinking and his failure to attend to minimal professorial business.

"Why was this malcontent incompetent appointed?"

"We needed to replace a retiring colleague who specialized in the literature of the American South. We had a poor field of candidates. There were perky New Yorkers ready to find Jewish humor in the wit and wisdom of Dr. Johnson; aggressive Canadians ready to make *Othello* relevant to the prairies; and Midwesterners ready to hone their American Stage English near New York.

"Then there was this little gray man who had not one, but two Ph.Ds: one from Columbia, one from Oxford. It was his success at Columbia with a Ph.D on "Prophecies in Shakespeare's Histories" that earned him a graduate scholarship to Oxford where he turned to the subject of "Burning Witches in English Literature." Neither Ph.D was on literature of the South. Nevertheless, his mother hailed from the New South. Then, his late stepfather was Warren Burns, our most famous scientist, whose family home was right in the midst of the Milhous community."

When the chair of the English Department mentioned that this house was located in Milhous Avenue where all the other buildings except Holy Cross Church and the Burns mansion belonged to Milhous College, Groznyy's eyes hardened with a Fagin-like gleam as he set his mind racing to acquisition. But the chair did think it odd that the provost should have calmed down with a declaration to work things out with Bedfellow Burns.

Groznyy saw a way to raise his status and put a cat—no, a tiger—among the scurrying pigeons of Milhous College. First, get the house. Then, make its facade the front for aggressive new buildings for BCU. It would be right in the middle of the damned Milhous College.

Whatever his salary while he was rising in academia, Groznyy had always set aside funds for rental property investment with old lawyer chum Larry Dawdler. Dawdler had the jutting chin and assertive expression of a former college jock whose broad frame could carry the weight of middle-aged spread. He still cut an attractive figure. When Groznyy consulted him about the Bedfellow Burns house, he cautioned him.

"You won't get away with it," he said, "Zoning regulations won't allow it. Milhous will move heaven and earth to prevent your invasion of its most prestigious street."

"We'll see about that," answered Groznyy with smiling insistence.

*

30

Ashley Bedfellow Burns had not sobered up when he faced the provost while shivering in his shoes. He thought there would be accusations about his teaching. He was taken off his guard when Groznyy took a different tack.

"Do you enjoy my speeches? Do you think I speak well?"

"Yes. Everyone says how dexterous and insightful your words are."

"Come now, there's your mother."

"My mother?"

"Your mother—the little lady with the big blue eyes—Beth Helene isn't it?—your mother on the front row. She had the nerve to say afterwards that my wife was getting thinner and thinner. When someone corrected her, she said that perhaps I was getting fatter and fatter."

"I think she may have said 'faster.'" Then Ashley added with candor, "She's an old lady. She says what comes into her head. No self censorship."

"You censor her. You cut her down to size. Button up her lips."

"She's a timid old lady."

"Then it'll be all the easier for you to cow her. The old heifer. Her ankles are giving birth to calves. I don't want to see her around."

"You and me, both," thought Ashley, but he was shocked at the provost's change of tone.

Then the stick disappeared and it was back to the carrot.

"Your family has a long distinguished association with the university through your stepfather and your house. Surely the house is too big for your needs, too inconvenient for your little old lady mother? I know you are not well. Your students and your departmental colleagues have made formal complaints about your drinking, about your coming to classes late, the reek of alcohol on your breath, your very red face with its pustules, and your not grading papers. You are coming up for tenure, aren't you?"

Ashley nodded. He realized where this was leading.

"Alcoholism is a sickness. The university health plan recognizes this. Here is my constructive suggestion. I will use my advocacy so that you can get the best treatment for your condition. You won't need your accommodation here while you are in rehab. I will make the best possible account of your case when it comes to the trustees' decision about your tenure. The university has plans, big plans, and they include real estate development. We will purchase your house at a fair market price, rename it after your esteemed stepfather, and develop it as an imposing facade for new university buildings on the grounds of your extensive garden. In this way, we all win. You get the supportive treatment you need and respite from teaching. You get tenure and, with investment, you get a generous annuity for the rest of your life."

Groznyy was not only enjoying the malign power play in which he had the upper hand but he was also getting a perverse satisfaction in both anticipating and feeling the acute pain that Ashley would undergo in his downward spiral into greater alcoholism.

"Your stepsister gets funds for her daughters' college education. There will be extra funds for your mother to enjoy her senior years in the best possible retirement home. Through my contacts, I can make an appropriate recommendation; probably The Gateway, three towns over, in which I have invested my own retirement funds—so that's a guarantee of quality."

Ashley was cornered and he knew it. It was a done deal and he knew that, too. He wanted his professorship more than he needed the house. So he took the money and ran. That left the immediate problem of his sojourning mother. On this he and his stepsister were united.

Thus did Ashley step onto a descending escalator to ruin as a victim of the modern Ivan, a hapless cog caught in devilish machinations.

*

None of the three players in the next scenario—the same villain but another mother and son—knew how their awkward situation would also develop into tragedy. This mother and son were Groznyy's present wife and his own son and heir. This wife and son did sense remorseless time hastening them to a future more disturbing than their troubled present.

Once they were installed in the Bedfellow Burns house, Anna Stasinova, Groznyy's wife, understood why Groznyy had coveted it. The downstairs hall was Gothic in style and circular with four great doors besides the imposing entrance. To her, each door seemed ominous, representing not an opening but a closing that denied any chance of happiness.

The first door was shut. The second door was ajar. Anna heard a tap dripping in the kitchen. When it started to rain heavily, it was as if the provost's new house was crying, somehow reasserting the rights of its previous owners and its own independent character.

Anna watched silently from the half-open door as Groznyy played his nightly game of chess against himself, using a table with a swivel top so he could change sides with a flick of his wrist. He passed over each and every piece, salivating over the power he felt by promoting, demoting, and destroying his pawns. She found his habit of sucking the tips of the pieces—the monarchs' crowns, the horses' manes, and the castle battlements—even more sickening than before. From time to time Groznyy fondled a pawn, moistening it with his lips, like a toddler sucking a nipple.

Groznyy had expected that Franklin Miller would micro manage his every act as provost. That's what he would have done. But no. Miller was often away. But it was not on fund-raising business. He usually said he was going to Vienna in Fairfax County in Virginia, just outside Washington, D.C.

33

Groznyy assumed this was so that Miller did not have to say he was going to Langley, also in Fairfax County, and known as the base of the CIA. With the duke away, his deputy—Groznyy—was expected to run everything smoothly. But then—damn him—when he least expected it, Miller would be back.

Groznyy knew he would need legal help in the murky political environment of little BCU. He had started to build up his property portfolio along with his old college chum, the attorney Larry Dawdler. He appreciated Dawdler's business acumen and his deference to Groznyy's seductive charm. When the principal lawyer for BCU retired, Groznyy created a new post of attorney general to entice Dawdler into work at BCU to serve him.

To shield himself further Groznyy had his own psychological bunker. Its center was a Kitchen Cabinet that included Dawdler. The rest were functionaries, such as Lorraine Boe, director of Human Resources.

Warm-hearted Italian American Lorraine Boe admired both Miller and Groznyy. Their surface courtesy, their skill with words, and their special way of wining and dining their guests and their office pets made her head spin round and round. It was all so stylish in comparison with what she now knew had been the dreary dullards who had previously come to BCU as president and provost. It was the sense of style of Miller and Groznyy that struck her heart with admiration leading to adulation.

But nothing satisfied the new provost. Every evening in the Groznyy house it was always the same game of chess. Anna left the lights off in the main room. The only light came through the second door still ajar and beyond it, the other two doors in the hall. From the upstairs window, Long Island Sound looked both nearer and smaller—as if it was a lake of tears. All Anna had to live for now was Modest.

Groznyy's son by Anna, named Modest, was lively and boisterous. Modest was a youngster who lived for the natural world of hills and dales, brooks and trees. While his father's dark university world was petty power politics, as a child, Modest's fair outdoors world was fun-and-games with pet animals. Modest was always untidy, always late—even for meals for which he had a healthy appetite.

When he was an infant, Groznyy used to caress Modest's curls and whisper loving words as he read Pushkin to him in Russian. But a sad turning point came when his anxious parents learned that Modest was very short-sighted and that his eyesight would get worse. Groznyy now shrank from touching him. His narcissism stifled any parental affection. Modest needed ever-thicker eyeglasses. And Groznyy loathed these Coke-bottle glasses. He called Modest "Four Eyes."

In his impotent rage of revulsion that Modest was now physically imperfect, Groznyy would threaten him whenever he did something grown-ups might think mischievous. And whenever Anna did something he considered defiance over a household trifle, he would grab her lower face and twist it as a sign of displeasure for conceiving an impaired child.

His father complained that Modest was too true to his name—too bashful, too unassuming. Larry Dawdler chided Cesare for being unreasonable: "Chief, go easy on the kid. What would your reaction be if you had named him 'Valiant' or 'Charming,' since no one is expected to be as valiant, as charming, as seductive, as you?"

However, Groznyy could think of Modest as an extension of himself, since Modest had a budding, outsize talent that he reluctantly admired because of his love of art. In his purchases from Soho galleries, Groznyy championed modern art in general and abstract expressionism in partic-ular. Anna Stasinova thought Groznyy's obsession had started in World War II, with his seeing so many distorted mangled limbs and so many distended corpses. That was why he appreciated the depiction of man's inhumanity to man by such artists as Ben Shahn and Peter Blume. This, in turn, led him to appreciate the shattering effects of abstract expressionism.

Modest could draw. His thumbnail sketches, achieved spontaneously, summed up his subjects in a few deft strokes. Modest's hand-held crayon passed over a sheet of paper. Then, *voila*, it was done: a series of affectionate cartoons of the professors Cesare worked with. At Babel City University they were minor masterpieces. Knowing this was a skill Groznyy could not possibly emulate hurt him even more.

Worse, within his uneasy relationship with his son and heir lay a paralyzing fear. Groznyy knew that Modest's regressive eye condition was essentially congenital. He blamed Anna. He dreaded ever being told that it came from him. He took out his inner rage on all sorts of people and things disabled: deaf people, visually impaired people, amputees, medical specialists, even enabling equipment such as magnifying glasses, hearing aids, and wheelchairs. He was appalled to discover that BCU had a battery of what he termed "hen professors" and technical assistants in a department of speech pathology.

Anna realized that all three of them—father, mother, and son—were trapped in a tunnel of Groznyy's devising. When Groznyy was out of town her evening escape was into tumultuous love affairs in romantic operas on her LPs. When Groznyy was in town, Anna's afternoon escapes came in TV soaps, especially those wherein power women Stephanie Forrester in *The Bold and the Beautiful* and Lucinda Walsh in *As the World Turns*, manipulated themselves into and out of situations both benevolent and malign. Anna knew she had neither the emotional courage nor the economic means to escape. So she focused ever more on Modest: his education, his future, and his safety. Anna and Modest had selfless love for one another.

During his tender boyhood Anna would watch Modest eat his child's lunch. He sat at a table opposite a cabinet with glass doors. Modest would look up and smile at his reflection in the glass. This comforted Anna. She understood that Modest must have escaped the hatred she and Groznyy felt for one another. Modest liked himself and he liked the world. His first favorite song was "Wonderful World," especially if Louis Armstrong was singing. From there he developed a love for jazz that would sustain him through the ultra-tense atmosphere at home.

Anna herself was often sick with a menu of ailments. In case she did not survive, she planned an escape hatch for Modest. She knew that Princess Glinskaya owed Groznyy for helping her to launch her niche restaurant. Anna summoned her failing courage to call Groznyy's formidable relative. She explained Modest's condition and the doctors' advice. Would the princess kindly let Modest come and see her in New York from time to time? The very act of traveling to New York by himself would give him skills and confidence if the light ever dimmed in his eyes.

To her surprise, the princess agreed readily. After Modest's first enjoyable visit when he charmed the princess, Anna knew she had guessed correctly. She said to herself, "Once Modest makes friends with you, you are his for the rest of your life." Modest's winning ways would open whatever doors Benny and the princess could manage when the time arose.

Groznyy realized that Modest disturbed him more and more. Everyone found his friendliness infectious. Groznyy wanted to be feared across the university. He succeeded. This success came with a penalty. That the professors and their families who knew Modest preferred him was gall in

Groznyy's mouth. It seemed to descend through his inner pipes and coruscate his innards. The one thing he did not want to do was to loathe himself. The more this feeling grew, the more he saw Modest being adored and the more he began to fear him. Was it hate? Was it self-doubt? Cesare resented Modest's vigor. He resented his abundant hair— "more than he knows what to do with"—what he called Modest's "cascade of corkscrew curls."

In the restaurant, Benny was surprised that it had come so quickly.

"Like the song says, it's time for me to adjust to my age, to sit back and take it easy," said the princess. "I cannot teach you anything more. You're better than me already. I haven't the energy for New York like I used to have. I shall retire to the country. Don't look surprised. There's a retirement home in Pickaway County in New England. The brochure makes it look delightful."

The princess handed Benny a brochure.

"And I have a guarantee. My great nephew in all but name is one of the owners. It's in his portfolio. So I'm assured of a happy, painless sunset. You stay here and run things as beautifully as you have so far, caro Benny, with the prospect of having it all when I'm no longer here."

What Benny said was, "You're too kind." What he thought was, "She loves to keep us all guessing, wishing, and hoping for the future."

Upstairs, Benny was bored. Instead of the gourmet heaven of cross-dressing chef Imelda's delicacies two floors below, in his city heights third floor, Benny Vincenzo preferred fast food cheeseburgers dripping with ketchup. When he had first started at the Golden Cockerel, he was a slightly podgy six-footer whom well-cut dinner jackets could transform into a stylish and mature manager. But in his first six months as sole boss, released from all constraints of budget and even the minimal exercise of walking ten blocks to work, he first blossomed into 300 pounds then, within eighteen months, ballooned into near 400 pounds of super-stately sloth.

In his apartment, on his super-ample chaise longue, he would loll over endless snacks while gorging himself intellectually on dramatic bonbons of Public TV's *Masterpiece Theatre* and *Mystery.* There were their imports of British television adaptations of English novels to emphasize Theme Park UK. That might be the stately homes of England beautifully dressed for costume dramas with surprising all-year-round sunshine. It might also be all the clichés of smoke-stacked, fog-swirling pollution for the Industrial Revolution or the harshest terrors of urban street-crime stereotypes for TV noir.

Before she left for New England and blissful retirement, the princess had suggested to Benny that he take up a hobby that would keep him more safely at home than his dangerous nocturnal encounters in hustler bars. It would also satisfy his mania for collecting while giving rich expression to his stifled artistic vein. When he was a lad, Benny Vincenzo had loved playing with his sister's dolls' houses. For hours he would toy with the little furniture and human beings he moved around them and whom he named "the tinies."

Unlocking the child in the outsize body of the grown man, the princess had suggested Benny start his own collection of special historical rooms. He could begin by commissioning some "resting" stage designer in Manhattan to construct a setting into which he could place people, furniture, and *objets d'art* acquired from catalogs. To persuade him, she went with him three blocks west to the Henry Villard houses, then a frontispiece for a Helmsley Palace Hotel.

While the exterior was based on a Roman Renaissance palazzo, the Villard interiors were based on the French

Renaissance. They boasted work by nineteenth-century American designers. For the Gold Room artist John LaFarge had painted murals depicting Music and Art. The princess persuaded Benny to make a miniature version of this room, recreating it, and to buy minute tables and chairs, chandeliers and pictures to furnish it.

So, upstairs Benny now lay or crouched at his toy theater's remembrance of things past, moving the diminutive chairs and armchairs, mock chandeliers, and postage-stamp size Goya tapestry cartoons, slotting them into dwarf settings as surely as a medical specialist in keyhole surgery.

Encouraged by his first artistic success, Benny's ideas grew grander. The princess then suggested he plan a room with greater impact, based on something dear to American hearts.

"Don't choose something obvious—another Manhattan house or even a mansion in Newport. For God's sake, choose something different."

They both decided on the same model—the reception room of a much-photographed mansion on Milhous Avenue aside the great Milhous College in New England, a road begun after the Civil War when poets called it the most beautiful street in America.

This design would help back a murderer into a corner.

COLLATERAL DAMAGE

Beth Helene Bedfellow could hear the woman in the next bed complaining—always complaining. It was after supper one October evening. Beth was still frail, recovering from a late summer cold.

"I need the bedpan," sang her neighbor. "Quickly, nurse. It's coming out. Jesus Christ, help me. I can't stop it."

Beth could hardly bear the smell. She wondered how gaga she would have to be not to notice the stinking odor. She lay on her side and scrutinized the comatose forms of the other two ladies in the four-bed room. One was breathing heavily. The other was silent in another world.

Even though night was falling, Beth rose and tried to concentrate on the view through the window—lovely cherry trees, probably beautiful blossom in May—pink, refulgent, and adorable-smelling. Although she was in New England, it reminded her of something she had never experienced herself, the fairytale charm of the Old South, the legend her very own grandmother had whispered to her as a child. It was the fairy tale immortalized by writer Margaret Mitchell of a civilization "Gone with the Wind." Beth had named her son Ashley after one of the famous novel's unattainable heroes. But, much as she hankered after the spring blossoms, she hoped she would not see them.

Beth hated the smell of dung and urine in the home. It was named "The Gateway" but that did not fool the residents abandoned by their families. It was a gateway, all right, and a vestibule of never-ending purgatory of decay by smell—burial before you really were dead. Thus the oblivion of death, as preachers said, would be a merciful relief. Relief? Could she relieve herself? The poor dear in the next bed had relieved herself in *her* bed. Now the whole wide world knew about it—everyone but the care assistants in The Gateway.

Beth had come to the home for retired folks most reluctantly. She loved her much-gabled house with its spires and turrets, its three winding staircases, its dark panels, even the blue outside lights that ensnared summer moths. Each time Ruth, her married stepdaughter, had visited her and a moth met its end and a light sizzled, Ruth always said the same thing: "Snap! Another bug has gone to meet his maker," and slapped her ample thighs.

Beth had loved her impossible-to-manage house not just because it had been her home ever since her second marriage but also because it was a comfortable, easy home with floppy armchairs. It housed her past.

There was the garage-cum-shed with her second husband's tools. There were the cases with Ashley's books from Columbia and from Oxford.

Her bedside table had trinkets next to the lamp. The family had always seen frugality as a virtue. Beth did not discard used magazines. She cut magazines into strips—shredded them they would say now. Beth knew some gym lingo from her step granddaughters through Ruth. Having shredded the magazine pages, she took gray paste from a jar and splashed it across the strips of paper. Then she twisted the strips tightly to make coils like the braids of a young girl's hair, tighter and tighter till the coils were neat. Finally she left them to dry, hanging from the porch windows like gay streamers.

When the streamers were completely dry, she harvested them, gathered them in their string forms, and mixed two or three together to make choker necklaces. Everyone said how lovely they were. They were always popular at sales for the church. And she felt useful making them. The nicest thing was the surprise of the unexpected array of colors—how a magazine picture that seemed mainly teal in color would in globular pearl strings suddenly show surprising indigo or maroon coloring.

But she was back to the future.

When an orderly appeared, Beth, now sitting on her bed in The Gateway, gasped anew at the stench of bowels opened into not-so-clean sheets.

"Lula Belle, what you been doin', dirtying yourself? Got a rocket up your ass, honey—or out of it?"

"I couldn't help it," said the old lady. "It was the hospital investigation with the tube down my throat lookin' for kidney stones. The hospital should've known it was too dangerous for me. I'm eighty-eight, ya know. The pain is extreme. They only found tiny, tiny pebbles, tiny kidney stones."

"We haven't time for that now. Let's get you cleaned up, instead of stinking the whole house down."

The care assistant heaved herself over to the window and, with another heave, got it open. To Beth the air was refreshing, if biting. Then the care assistant produced a wadge of paper towels with which she began wiping down her elderly charge. The old lady was stripped from the waist down.

"Let's get you hosed down in the shower."

The bed was stripped and the sheets taken away. But not the blanket. That was wiped summarily with the paper towels.

When Lula Belle—for that was what the care assistant in her fanciful way called the offending resident—returned, she was told, "No more clean sheets till tomorrow. Sleep on the blanket or underneath it. Don't complain. Don't fret. Morning will come soon enough."

For Beth it was all so different from how her son, Ashley, and her stepdaughter, Ruth, had presented her move from comfortable Norse Hoven to The Gateway in Pickaway County.

First, they had begun dropping hints that Beth was getting forgetful. She would cook a southern dinner perfectly but forget about the rice or the biscuits until it was too late. She would draw her bath perfectly but then forget and leave the water running. She would forget her pocketbook.

In this scenario, the house was forgetful, too. It forgot its clapboards needed repair. It forgot to exchange lower window panes for screens in summer and it forgot to change them back again for winter. It forgot it was no longer young and that it needed constant repair—renovation, really—and that it could not afford, anyways.

With her son working too hard as a college professor and her stepdaughter a few towns away concentrating on her own three daughters and their coming children, there was no room in their lives for Beth.

"We're only thinking of you. The house is too big for you—correction—for any of us to manage. Adapting a mansion like that for a little old lady, no matter how sweet, would cost a fortune. Maybe even a million couldn't do it. Now we can sell it. There'll be enough money to pay for your proper care plus something extra for your three grand-daughters as they set up on their own with their partners."

"We've found this lovely retirement home, just three towns away. We can visit whenever we—correction— whenever you like."

The Gateway would allow Beth to keep a handful of diminutive possessions. Along with family photos of her two late husbands, herself, and the children as teenagers, she had brought two oval miniatures of eighteenth-century Gainsborough-type beauties, heads and shoulders with elaborate powdered hairstyles. Beth knew they were really early twentieth-century copies of older paintings, both set in oblong frames of yellowed ivory panels culled from old piano keys. But she loved them, nevertheless.

There was also Beth's favorite childhood doll—her only doll—a black lady of soft material, with, to Beth, charming features and southern clothes. This was Biddy, her adored companion across the US. Her stepdaughter wondered about banning this doll because it would surely offend some care workers at The Gateway. But since her priority was to get Beth out of her hair, she wanted to avoid anything to arouse Beth's suspicions about where she was going. Ruth

44

had heard about an old exposé documentary film about scandalous treatment of inmates at a home for mentally ill people in New England: *Titicut Follies*. Because she did not want to provoke a temper tantrum, Ruth kept her mouth buttoned up.

Once installed at The Gateway, Beth learned to hate the old people's home, the insincerity of the smiling staff, the stale-sweat atmosphere, and the periodic cruelty of the manager. The hours seemed endless but, somehow, days passed into weeks. Her life was drifting away. Yet, unexpectedly, one day in this vestibule to hell she found a savior of sorts.

When Beth first met Princess Glinskaya, it was love at first sight.

There she sat in a leaf-green armchair with immaculately coiffed silver hair. She was wrapped in a glistening cashmere shawl, turquoise with a red and black pattern and a seam of gold running through its woof and warp. Where Beth decorated her modest tops with her home-made necklaces, Princess Glinskaya was content with nothing less than shards of gleaming costume jewelry, baubles large enough to reflect light from the windows by day and the ceiling lights at night. She was like royalty. When she moved, she swayed like a temptress in a Hollywood B movie.

"Come close, my child," she whispered to Beth, despite the fact that Beth must have been her age or even older. She almost lisped with an accent that Beth could not think was real. Was it Russian? Was it French?

"Come close, dear child. If you have something deliciously wicked to say about someone, sit close to me."

While she spoke, the princess would cross her legs. In case this allowed immodest glimpses of her stockinged thighs, she would adjust her black flared skirt down. But a moment later she would shift herself in the chair slightly so that the skirt was raised again. Once again, the crossing of legs disclosed lissom limbs ready for some unspecified, tempting action.

45

Now the princess was off in her imagined life in an art-world Russia that had never truly existed. It was a world of mammoth altar walls studded with icons, walls that were like outsize stage sets; a world with golden steppes under endless azure skies; of onion domes painted all colors of the rainbow; an art world so different from the failing Soviet Union with its bludgeoned stone figures of Mr. and Mrs. Russia bringing in the wheat or harvesting the hides. The princess hated such monumental statues, giants of supposed industrial progress that dominated public buildings in the USSR. The statues' eyes were fixed on the never-never future of a state withered away and oblivious to the pain of past and present sacrifices.

If Princess Glinskaya ever referred to such dark Soviet matters, these black holes in the torn fabric of the Iron Curtain, she spluttered with her indeterminate European accent her hatred of all things communist: the degradation of people; the blunting of classes; the brutal bending of music and art to serve a series of bigoted tyrants. Any cult of personality she wanted was not for Soviet despots but for him she called her great relative.

"My nephew, adopted in all but name, is a famous academic leader of educational reform like your own son of Virginia, Woodrow Wilson, working for the greater good of human beings everywhere. Famous and learned."

Beth was not sure if this was real. But she was fascinated nonetheless.

What Princess Glinskaya had said was far from her real opinion of Groznyy and he was not yet a college president but she kept that to herself since family loyalty was important. Besides, to create an aura of power around her in the outer world was paramount. However, the pretentiousness of her statements aggravated other residents in the home and, more significantly, the care workers.

"Princess, my eye! She's no more a princess of royal blood

than I am," said the help who had stripped Lula Belle of all dignity in the stinking bedroom.

"She's a fake through and through. That accent! Those clothes! Those affectations! It's like Queen Marie of Romania—came to New York—oh! decades ago. Gave herself such airs. Got into New York society and made the rounds. Ran circles round the Rockefellers and Vanderbilts. But no one really knew who she was or where she came from. That's just like our precious princess.

"She's taken her cue from old movies, from character actresses hankering after best supporting Oscars. You know what I heard? That she used to live just outside Moscow in a suburb, in a hideous tower block that would make any US projects look like the Palace of Versailles.

"And how did she earn her crusts? The clues are in her bedside cabinet. I've seen them. I've been through her things: icons, Russian icons. She used to paint icons for foreign tourists. Princess? Give me a break!"

With that, the first care assistant popped a grape from a resident's bedside bowl into her eager mouth. She swallowed it without chewing. The second assistant thought she might see it slide down her neck like a giraffe swallowing an orange whole.

Resuming her tirade, the first assistant became more intimate in her critique.

"Look at those orange cheeks."

"I think her color does change, naturally."

"Yes, when she changes the Max Factor pots."

"Benny," lisped the princess when she called the restaurant after lunch. "I'm at a payphone in the town. I've made a terrible mistake. I'm not ashamed to admit it. It's a hell hole: the filth, the rudeness, and such bovine people. You have to get me out of here without Groznyy knowing. I'll make it worth your while."

*

47

Two days after the little domestic mishap in the resident's bed, the overseer of The Gateway blamed innocent Beth for the calamity of incontinence.

"I blame you. Lula Belle has been ill. You should've called for help earlier—not waited for the mini explosion of excrement. I think your evening drink of Spanish sherry with the princess is the cause. Besides, you've only just got over a heavy cold. Let's get you back to teetotal, family values. Let's clear your chest. We don't want you catching your death. No evening drink for a week. You can have hot milk to calm you.

"And another thing, you're living in the past, madamina. There's no place for an English golliwog here."

With that, the overseer plucked the offensive item, Biddy, from the bedcover with two disdainful fingers and deposited her in a garbage bag conveniently poking out of her apron pocket.

Beth knew that once a little girl grew up she left her dolls behind. Then, the light within the dolls was no more, extinguished. Their souls shriveled. No one believed in them and they died. Was this to be her fate?

Beth felt the sap of the distasteful evening meal rising. It was all she could do to stop herself throwing up. She broke down before the princess and explained how she had come to this sorry situation, how a wicked provost had manipulated her dear son into selling their college home from right under her. Because of her tears and her frustration, Beth did not notice the princess's eyes widen at her grief.

She felt that someone was singing outside her open window. But surely that could not be the case? She had always thought that the sky at night was magical as indigo turned into midnight black. As it became black that evening, it seemed to her to sigh like a lament for her youth long faded away.

She lay motionless in bed that night, not through sleep but because she had started to plan ahead.

She thought that the tumbledown house three towns over had not yet been sold. There had been a buyer—a front for the wicked provost—who wanted to use it as the frontispiece for a flotilla of surrounding university buildings. But there had been—or so she thought—some snafu over planning because the house was in a famous spacious avenue of college houses—something about conflict with zoning regulations—and the scheme had stalled. That was what her stepdaughter had told her.

Beth would return. She would tell Ashley and her stepdaughter how terrible was her present existence, divorced from decency. She would tell them how she missed them, her family, whom she loved, and how she wanted to be back in her beloved home. Surely they would see and understand, if they heard it from her own lips? And if the big house was to be converted, nevertheless, then she, Beth, could live in one of the new subdivided apartments in the old house. As Beth planned her escape, the mere thought of it eased her mind— even banished the smell. She sensed a smile flicker across her face as she closed her eyes for sleep, thinking of her son and stepdaughter as youngsters gamboling in the fields.

Next day, following her decision, Beth heard the help talking in the morning shift as they cleaned the corridors.

"My favorite meerkat is May Belle; she's polite and refined."

"Yeah. But Pocket Frog has more pizzazz, know what I mean?"

"Well, whatever their traits—minus and plus—those meerkats and the other two—Frump Ass and Broccoli Flower—they just don't get along. The chemistry sure ain't right."

"That's 'cos there's no alpha female among this particular quartet to keep order."

"You can say that again. What about the phony princess next door?"

"Don't make me laugh. She can always be relied upon to cause a stink in more ways than one."

This was followed by a double guffaw. It made Beth start. To begin with she had thought the care assistants must have been talking about household pets. Now she realized that she and the other residents were the meerkats. The help considered them animals. It was she and her companions who were May Belle and Lula Belle, Frump Ass and Broccoli Flower. They despised the princess whom Beth adored. The shame of it!

This is what she had come to. Surely, for all their minor differences, her stepdaughter would never have consented to this degradation. When Beth had been a little girl and done something her folks considered the tiniest bit naughty, they had told her that children who went to the bad were sent to hell after they died. She had heard of hellfire in sermons. But never could she have imagined hell on earth. This was hell, wasn't it? She was still alive, wasn't she? Were they trying to drive her mad so that she didn't know the difference between life and death? She pulled herself together.

Once when she had been chatting with Curra, the most reassuring care assistant, she had asked, "Do you live in the town nearby?"

"No, honey. Two towns over. Takes two buses. The bus company isn't state-wide when it comes to services between towns. I have to get one bus four blocks from my home through the town center and then get off at a terminus by a shopping mall. Then I get me another bus to bring me here. Takes the best part of ninety minutes. Your folks live another bus ride, another stage of the journey, over."

For no reason Beth could think, she had treasured—yes, treasured—this information. Now it hit her sharply. And she still had enough wit to use it. But she had no funds. Everything was tied up in her rent and board.

Beth had seen Curra eye the two miniatures-in-ivory atop her cabinet.

"You like them, don't you, dear?"

"Yes, ma'am."

"They were valued by Sotheby's—the auctioneers."

"Well, I could pay you for them. Ten dollars up front. Then ten dollars for one this week; ten dollars, next, for the second. Thirty dollars altogether."

"It's a done deal."

Curra gave Beth a ten-dollar bill.

Later that same day Curra gave Beth another ten-dollar bill. Then she wrapped up one miniature in toilet paper and took it away with her.

Twenty dollars would be enough for the journey, surely. If not, Beth would have the second miniature to hand. She kissed it before she wound it back in another hastily made toilet-paper shroud.

As she noticed Beth's unusual action, Princess Glinskaya, unexpectedly standing in the doorway, said simply, "My child, dear one, you are like my other self."

Beth was startled. Had the princess guessed her secret plans?

"Do not worry. I'm with you. Let's do it together. How do you say in English, 'Two heads are better than one'?"

The princess realized Beth was pondering what to do.

"If I go with you to your house, dear one, and stay with you for one night, then, next day, I can get the Metro North train into the city."

Beth was in a quandary. Even if the princess was for real, would two heads really be better than one? Beth knew there would be advantages to being as inconspicuous as she was. Mousy, yes, that was the word. Just a sweet old lady: old, harmless. But Princess Glinskaya, while as nice and gracious as they could come, was hardly inconspicuous. What word would dear Ashley use? Flamboyant—yes, that was it. Then, Beth knew her own courage might fail her if she tried to do it alone. Yes, she would take the risk. Together, they would try. Together, they would succeed or fail.

She was thinking ahead. When they left, they would have to go in some disguise. What Beth was about to do, she had never done before. When her three companions were asleep, she opened their closet doors.

"Sweet Jesus, forgive me, I've never taken anything from anyone before. My need is great."

She took a coat, a woolen hat, and a scarf from her companions' shabby vestments.

"For disguise, dear Jesus," she whispered.

She remembered the princess and took a second coat and scarf.

Beth had been long enough at The Gateway to know the times of buses at the end of the short drive and how the carers' individual schedules were slotted around those of the bus company.

Next day at lunch, she finished her sandwich in the canteen, made polite excuses and went upstairs. She took the borrowed outdoor clothes she had hidden in her own closet and put them in a carrier bag.

There was a women's rest room downstairs. She left the second half-ensemble behind the cistern for Princess Glinskaya at 1:45 pm. Then she moved cautiously. It was like tiptoeing out. Her companions were scouring newspapers. The care officers were absorbed in housekeeping.

Beth got to the bus stop at the end of the curling drive. It was hidden from the house by bushes and trees. With trepidation, she put on her borrowed finery. The multicolored scarf looked garish but there was no going back to change. She waited for the bus. The suspense was killing.

Then, Princess Glinskaya appeared precisely at 2:00 pm. In her borrowed un-refinery, she looked like an outrageous plumed parrot.

Beth suggested that Princess Glinskaya took off her eye-catching costume jewelry and put it in her pocketbook. However, she knew the princess would feel naked without some jewelry so she gave her some of her own paper-made necklaces.

When the bus arrived, Beth assumed her most old-worldly southern charm to explain that these two old dears did not have the right, two-dollar amount for the bus fare. Could someone give them change for ten dollars and could the driver also give them a transfer for the second stage of the journey?

Everything went smoothly. As the bus bumped along sleepy roads, the bushes and trees seemed to say to her, "You're going home, you're coming home. Welcome, Beth. Welcome home."

Princess Glinskaya was in another world.

Beth knew what an interchange was so the passage from one bus to another was also easy enough.

"No problem," said the second driver. "No problem."

But when they came to the second interchange for the third bus, it was different. Beth felt people were looking at them. Had the hated home raised the alarm?

"Ladies, the next bus to Norse Hoven is two hours yet. Why don't you both get a soda from the machines, help pass the time?"

Beth knew if they stayed in the depot they would be discovered. Princess Glinskaya looked even more flamboyant in the grubby bus depot, a tawdry old bag lady who had lost her marbles. Beth knew they were both too tired to explore the little town. They walked a little and sat on a bench outside a cemetery near the town green. Somehow, it seemed comforting. Despite the Indian summer, the weather might suddenly change.

"Let's go in here. No one will think of looking for us in such a place," said Princess Glinskaya in her winning way. "Look, there are some Egyptian obelisks," continued the princess as if they were about to enter a faraway land. "Why, there's a student sketching them. Look, a boy with hyacinth curls, next to a Hispanic man with a sombrero."

As they moved inside, Beth stumbled. The gravestones seemed to threaten her as their shadows lengthened with the falling sun. She moved to another bench. When she looked round, she realized that Princess Glinskaya was gone. Beth was petrified.

"Why didn't you let us know earlier?" said stepdaughter Ruth when she took the call from the home.

"We're always here. We entrusted dear Beth to you. We told you about her problems—confusion, memory loss, and so on. But we also told you about her fiery independence. She came from the generation that got the ole U. S. of A. through the Great Depression. You let her down. You let us down."

"Yeah, yeah, yeah—and you might have mentioned she was a kleptomaniac. Would take anything—even the clothes off her neighbors' backs," answered the supervisor with the rolled-up garbage bag in her hip pocket.

"It's not a zoo. These residents are our guests. They can go into town. We've given the police photos and described Beth and the princess's outdoor wear. We have another hundred guests whom we love dearly. The world and its business don't stop here just because you can't cope with your own flesh and blood. No wonder they ran off together. Two old bats on the make and on the take."

This startled Ruth into submissive silence. Two old bats? What had happened to her damn stepmother? When she put down the handset, it was with more than a premonition of purgatory. Instead of being servile, the supervisor had been aggressive. The whole emphasis was on stepmother being in the wrong. Stealing clothes? That did not sound like stepmother either but that was what she had done. The Gateway's priority was not to find Beth. That fell to the police—how and when would depend on the police officers on duty. Beth had left the retirement home. Now, it was her family's problem. The old critter. Always in the way, except when she was needed.

Beth looked round the cemetery.

"My son is far away in college. It might as well be a distant land."

Now, nothing was worthwhile to her. Nothing mattered.

"Look, little lady," said a little girl holding her mother's hand. "You've dropped something."

"Thankee, kindly. It's a personal trifle."

Beth bent down to pick up the remaining ivory-encased miniature that she had dropped onto the red sandy path. It had got dirty as its tissue paper unfurled. She picked it up. She felt the miniature represented her heart, ready to be cut open by Death. Again, she took her place on the bench.

The grass of the untended lawns seemed to rustle, echoing the branches of the trees blowing in the autumn wind.

When Beth awoke, it was already dark. Without even looking at her wristwatch, she knew she must have missed the bus. She had no money for a hotel. If she went anywhere and asked questions, someone would identify her as the runaway from the hell home. Where was the princess? If they found Beth, she would have to go back to that house of shame. They would punish her in so many cutting ways. If you were not broken when you entered its fatal portals, the supervisor would break your spirit, kill your mind with unkindness and leave you with worn and grubby clothes propped up in an armchair like a discarded doll—like poor Biddy.

Beth was the modern Ivan the Terrible's second victim. Like her son, she began to understand her own tragedy though she never understood that Princess Glinskaya had also exploited her as if she were Groznyy's soul mate.

Beth dreaded the appearance of policemen in the guise of kindly escorts to escort her, convey her back to the dreadful tower of misery. She sensed there must be a brook nearby. She wanted a boat to come and waft her home. She realized that what was on her face was not the wetness of rain but her own involuntary tears.

For two hours Beth was cold but then she was so cold and wet that she ceased to notice as cold and wet and fear paralyzed her. This time, she lay down on the bench.

Autumn winds had blown away any lingering stubs of flowers and leaves. In her misery of cold and wind, Beth tried to concentrate on her youth decades earlier when she had first put out tendrils of tender emotion to her first fiancé. Now she longed for her children to comfort her. The brutal rustling of the trees seemed like heavy veils, like a drop curtain at the theater. When it was raised, when it opened, it would announce Death.

Before she sank into eternal sleep, Beth clasped some of the red sand of the path and looked upwards at the dark green boughs of the cemetery trees. Even at night she could make out their shapes. As the lesser limbs of the trees grew from the mighty branches, she fancied she saw them as holy crosses. Yes, they were crosses to her memory so that she would not be forgotten. If they ever thought this was suicide, this would be her grave marked by the natural crosses of the tree limbs. Their natural beauty would suffice as a scepter for her immortal soul.

In the morning a groundsman found her tumbled off her perch, a bundle of spent rags, a wasted doll. He knew this was another lost soul who had died of hypothermia. As she lay in pools of water left by a downpour, Beth looked like one of the wraiths of drowned girls, like a lake spirit of legend.

Out of grace, he touched Beth's almost frozen cheek. Out of almost-forgotten religious observance and respect for another human being, he crossed himself. In Beth's open eyes frozen in time, he seemed to detect a glimmer of fixed memory as to what life should be. He sensed that, however tortuous her death, no matter how degrading the plight that had brought this little lady here, her delicate frame held clues about the dignity of the human soul.

Later, they identified the unrecognizable old doll by her necklaces—her handmade treasures of paper strips playfully arranged with charming absentmindedness. But there was no Princess Glinskaya.

"Hypothermia caused by exposure," was the official verdict on Beth's death. The harsh phrase reverberated around the guilty family: abandoned because this family had placed its selfish interests before duty and care; abandoned like a homeless derelict, although they owed everything to her. Bitter were their tears of regret; bitter their explosive reproaches to one another as loveless stepdaughter shifted blame on to selfish son, and he shifted blame back to his self-interested stepsister and his errant nieces.

Even as they blamed everyone but themselves, they never thought to curse Ivan the Terrible in New England and the exotic, self-styled princess.

"Dear Beth," intoned the preacher at her funeral: "She represented the best of us, the best American values of steadfastness and compassion of an older generation steeped in courtesy."

Whatever lilies Ashley would scatter on Beth's grave would lacerate his soul. Now he could only face the future by drinking himself to the edge of oblivion. To Ashley, it was his mother who had been the best sentry of his life. It was she who had kept watch over his growing pains and cares, to whom he was handsome whereas he knew women found him physically repulsive and psychologically deformed.

When Death struck his mother, there was no way of turning back, no way of turning back the clock.

There were four of them at table in the upstairs dining room at the Golden Cockerel: Benny, the princess, Modest—the student with the hyacinth curls—and Bernardo, the head-waiter. Bernardo had driven Modest and the princess back from their meeting place, the cemetery in New England. Bernardo went downstairs to dispose of the sombrero.

"We don't need to do anything," said Benny. "Time and chance will come to your rescue. A woman's body will get washed ashore or found somewhere. The police will call Groznyy and he will be glad to identify it."

"If only to get his sticky fingers on my estate," the princess said. She was toying with the paper-shard necklaces Beth had given her.

"On the restaurant," Benny specified.

"We need to take precautions. I need to check the will, rewrite it, and, somehow, we need to get it predated," said the princess, still twisting and turning the necklaces.

"That can be arranged," continued Benny.

"But where do I go? Where do I hide? Be sure, if he knows I'm still here, he'll root me out."

Modest had it all worked out from his childhood books.

"Babushka, you can live secretly upstairs in the apartment next door above the delicatessen. There's a joining partition door on the fourth floor."

"But I'd be trapped, walled up."

"Not necessarily," continued ever-inventive Modest. "It's like *The Lion, the Witch, and the Wardrobe*. We place an English wardrobe in front of the partition door. When it's moved, or you pass through it, if we open up the back, you

58

have access this way to the restaurant. Next door, you have access to the street. You can come and go in all sorts of wrap-around clothes. You can be seen without being noticed. New York is cosmopolitan. No one really notices even if you go about in a burkha."

"I suppose it might work. At least, it will buy time," said Benny. "The lion, the witch, and the wardrobe malfunction. It's the sort of ruse gangsters on the run get up to."

The princess liked being compared to a gangster. She liked the ridiculous cloak-and-dagger scenario of her imaginative young relative. And she knew Modest would not betray her to his father. Benny was bemused. His agenda was to get control of the restaurant and prevent it becoming another of the finagling Groznyy's business interests. As he mixed them all drinks, he said under his breath, "The Liar, the Bitch, and the Wardrobe."

When the Babel City University board of trustees considered Ashley Bedfellow Burns's application for tenure, they agreed with the joint recommendation by department and provost: "DENIED on the grounds of lack of publications, inadequate teaching, and mental incompatibility."

"Not his fault," said Tiberius Brown, chair of the trustees. "Alcoholism may be a disease but it's also a social scourge. We cannot have the college infected."

In his brief early retirement, barroom regular Ashley would accost drinkers on adjacent bar stools or in the next booth. They might be treated to a harangue against the current American president, the current US foreign intervention somewhere or other, or the current Wall Street crisis. They might be chided for being unresponsive. Inevitably they complained to the bar management. Ashley found himself first being moved along, asked to leave others alone, or to leave that night, or to leave forever. The number of places he could frequent shrank.

*

59

At Babel City University the upshot of Groznyy's denial of expected tenure to Ashley and the suspicious death of his mother was faculty outrage. It manifested itself in widespread condemnation of Groznyy at meetings.

The aim of president and provost had been to transform Babel City University, to raise its academic standards. There were genuine progressive intentions amid the mayhem: to pare down department budgets to essentials so that there was parity between income and expenditure. However, professors were unwilling to accept the need for changes in teaching methods or to begin works of scholarship because this extra work would impinge on their fat cat lifestyles. They did not care about any adverse circumstances—that college enrollment was falling. That was for someone else to deal with. And in their minds, the shocking symbol of their justified grievance at Groznyy's exasperating needling of their standards was his cavalier treatment of Ashley—first the acquisition of his home, then his mother's suspicious death, and finally, his being denied tenure.

"Monstrous! He thinks he's another Ivan the Terrible of Russia."

This was how history professor Mordred Stickleman began his attack on Groznyy before a meeting of professors.

"Forget his early days of lavish receptions and even more lavish compliments to soften you up. Forget his forging tentative links with Ivy League universities. Once entrenched at BCU, the darker side of Groznyy's nature has emerged. It's like Tyrannosaurus Rex bursting through the foliage in Walt Disney's version of the *Rite of Spring*.

"We'd already heard on the academic grapevine about Groznyy's psychological torture of his colleagues elsewhere as he rose through the ranks. And at BCU we've learnt about Groznyy's mix of wheedling and scolding, his strategy of praising subordinates to the skies ahead of near-impossible deeds. Then comes his willful dissatisfaction that they had, indeed, been accomplished—these near miracles—but not as he wanted in some detail or because the glory went to the doer and not to him. So when the doers are exhausted, they get derided with scalding abuse.

"As an academic, never has he put pen to paper. Never has he worked through a scholarly idea nor dared set down any academic argument for peer review. With him, everything is surface verbal dexterity, littered with pretentious insights. But there's no substance behind the show."

Stickleman knew he had his colleagues' attention so he made his carefully prepared historical analogy:

"And now, his rule—for rule it is—well, the historical models are Henry VIII and Ivan IV, parallel despots of the Renaissance at either extremity of Europe—England and Russia. Henry VIII and Ivan IV—best remembered for their serial marriages—were tyrants who butchered family members and who took no prisoners in their feuds with the nobility.

"We have to stand firm against him—and now."

Stickleman was fueled by hate that he thought was righteous indignation. His academic rivals may have marveled at his oratory. While appreciating his pointed barbs, they guessed at his undying malice against Groznyy. As the senior professor in his department observed, "What Mordred says about people is very funny—except when it's you."

Stickleman knew he had not won over all hearts and minds on the day of his searing verbal attack on Groznyy. But something indefinable had shifted at BCU. The professors' irritation had morphed into discontent. It would coalesce into an opposition party.

By the time Groznyy took a phone call from Detective Leo

Guerra of the Norse Hoven Police he had already programmed himself to follow the princess's scenario without realizing that he was now her tool.

"Mr. Provost, we can't be sure but the police in New York have told us that an unidentified body has been recovered from the East River. It's an elderly female. I appreciate that this must be an unwelcome shock."

"However," began Groznyy, assuming a mask of contrition to cover his eager thoughts, "you would like me to identify the body?"

"Yes, sir, that sums it up."

He knew where to go. The morgue in New York where they had the mystery body was in Bellevue Hospital at 1st Avenue and 27th Street in Manhattan. Lit by harsh fluorescent lights, the hospital corridors were teeming with scurrying doctors and nurses, and shuffling patients and families tending IV trees trundling along on wheels.

The morgue itself was a capacious, refrigerated room. The walls wore an almost endless series of filing cabinets. The smell of chemicals was overpowering. The gloomy, antiseptic atmosphere helped Groznyy hone his consummate acting. He could adopt a show of controlled sadness.

On a silent cue from Leo Guerra, a morgue official curled his fingers around the metal handle of a drawer at waist height. He pulled out a bulging indigo garment bag closed by a coiled drawing thread. He tugged the zipper and peeled open the bag from top to sides.

To Groznyy's satisfaction, it was clear that all life had drained from the bloodless rubbery face. Groznyy did not recognize anything of the body as like the late princess, except that, maybe, the height and age were similar. But the body he saw had got swollen and distorted in the water. He had to think quickly since anything he said—fact or fiction—would restrict what he could say later. He hid his face from the officers, as if taking stock of his grief. They would not take a simple nod as sufficient affirmation. He had to say something—to identify the corpse in words.

Was it intentionally or not that the detective gave him a lucky break? He said, "It must be painful—difficult for us, too—because this person had a complete set of dentures and now they're gone, lost in the river."

Groznyy remembered that the princess also had a full set of dentures. There would probably be no other dental records. He decided to risk it.

"Yes, I think so. As you said, it's difficult because of the sea change in her. But I believe this is my dear great-aunt. May her soul rest in peace."

INSIGHT

The guest speaker at BCU was an ex-CIA man who wanted to wow the crowd. He gazed at a hall of expectant faces.

Because it was near New York, BCU, like Milhous and NHU, attracted speakers resident in, or visiting, Manhattan with books to promote or shows to plug. And the CIA man was one such. Todd Carter was a handsome guy. The cut of his features combined classic 1930s Hollywood matinee idol looks with a regular all-American clean-cut expression.

"After service in the marines where I was as patriotic as any red-blooded, all-American born-on-the-fourth-of-July-kind-of guy, I firmly believed in the impartial goodness of Uncle Sam. I needed no encouragement to join the CIA, set up after World War II to counteract the imperialist intentions of the communist bloc.

"I was naive. Science fiction with alien invaders—inspired by the Nazi or Soviet threat—convinced me it was my destiny to play my part in keeping America safe for democracy. When I joined the CIA, the Cold War was at its worst—subzero temperatures in diplomatic relations. But many political volcanoes were bubbling underground.

"After training, I was posted to a country in North Africa, above the Sahara. I won't name it—that would set us off at a tangent. One of the other CIA operatives there had been assigned to identify pockets of subversion in small towns. His task was to specify and assess the danger they posed to the existing regime and to us.

"My colleague drew a blank. The desert was indeed empty. The towns were quiet. The citizens were simply going about their daily business.

"When he reported this back to Washington—more correctly, to Langley, Virginia—they told him, 'That can't be. Look harder, man. The shit is everywhere. One day the dam of resentment will burst—demos, fireworks, uprising, embassies under siege, hostage takings, even massacres. And then, where will we be? You can be sure we'll get the blame. We should have known. We should have been ready. We should have anticipated it. Done something. Do something now, buddy. Otherwise, it's your job on the line.'

"For a day, my co-worker was baffled. Way back in Milhous College his undergrad major had been American literature. His minor had been modern history. So he knew about reading between the lines. His job on the line! He called another friend working in the Middle East."

"Another, 'My friend has problems,'" remarked Dean Ferrari to the man sitting next to him.

"His friend told him a similar tale. My colleague worked it out. He was a simple cog in the mighty CIA. It had offices and operatives across the world. Besides protecting US economic interests across the globe, it had to support its staff, expensively educated, meticulously trained—indoctrinated—all with superior skills of self-preservation. They have to be paid. And they have to earn their keep. Otherwise, they get canned.

"Now we come to the chicken nugget.

"What did my friend do? He had his family back home, mortgage to pay, kids going to college. The usual story.

"He thought long and hard. By now he was well connected with the local press. First he asked an editor, 'What about the guys who don't like your government, some with an ax to grind, some with a different political agenda from the current regime? What about them?'

"That phone call broke the wall of silence.

"'Yes,' answered the editor, 'some people think differently.'

"That phone call led to face-to-face meetings. My friend suggested—implied—that his newfound contacts should do something about their disagreements. 'Why not create a cell? We can help.' And help them my friend did. The cell became a nucleus of discontent, a secret cadre. It justified the CIA's suspicions. And it justified my friend's existence in Africa."

"And your point is?" asked Mordred Stickleman from the front row.

"Great organizations, great industrial companies and banks, may have their charismatic leaders, their presidents—national or commercial. But, once formed, these organizations also have their own momentum. Their managers and individual workers sustain them. These groups have their own agendas. And these include self preservation."

"What's the downside?"

"The downside is that we may think of the CIA as having US national interests at heart. However, its operatives generate those interests, create the target, and intentionally foment unrest in part to sustain themselves."

"I suppose you have a book to sell?" asked Dean Ferrari.

A hitherto unnoticed young man appeared on the platform and spoke.

"Yes. It's called *What's Wrong with the CIA*. Mr. Carter will be pleased to sign copies at the end of his presentation."

"Let me introduce my colleague. This is Mickey Garnier—my ghost-writer—and I'm not ashamed to admit it. Mickey, take a bow."

Stickleman was not going to let them get away with anything. He said, "I suppose the corollary of Mr. Carter's argument is that, if the CIA foments cadres of opposition parties in foreign countries, it can also play those opposition cards against sovereign governments when it thinks it will suit US interests to oppose a regime."

"You said it," said Todd Carter, as if it had been a compliment.

"And you left because?"

"I left because I could not look myself in the mirror while I was part of an organization that disrupted the political order in other countries simply to justify its existence economically."

"So, you were fired?"

Silence.

President Franklin Miller had let himself in quietly. He stood immobile at the back of the hall. What he heard alarmed him because Todd Carter's sort of subversion of the CIA might attach itself to his own reputation and prevent his becoming an ambassador. His mind raced ahead. He began to think how he could turn Todd Carter back to the good ship *US Patriot*.

Miller knew that if he could bring Carter with his handsome appearance and engaging style back into the fold, he would make an ideal front man to represent any government agency. True, the CIA would never have him back. But he could be turned all the same. For Corporate America and Communications America could hone his special skills to their advantage. He could become an American icon. He had fought in Vietnam and lived to tell the tale. Despite appearances, he was not WASP but German and Czech. He had charisma. And Miller thanked God for a welcome, humanizing touch. It seemed that Carter had a younger disabled sister to whom he was devoted. Turning Carter would be straightforward. After all, he could not stay an angry young man forever. After his fifteen minutes of fame, he would have to go back to earning a regular wage.

Dean Ferrari's neighbor at the talk by the former CIA man had been his guest. This was Don Fatale, a soft-spoken, squat African American with a shaved head, eyes that never overlooked anything, and a memory that forgot no one. His father had once belonged to the Nation of Islam, the Black Muslims, but left after the assassination of Malcolm X. Later, he and his wife had run a successful hardware store on West 125th Street, New York, so they could afford to send young Don to Rutgers where he majored in chemistry before going for his Ph.D at Harvard.

In Cambridge, Massachusetts, Don Fatale developed his other talent as a stage director and this took over his life. For, when it came to theater—especially musicals—young Fatale could conjure up a world of arresting color and movement that was not only ingenious but also achieved at minimal expense. A man standing on a chair and juddering while lit by strobe lighting could symbolize a victim of lynching in the American South. Two men bent forward with their backs to the audience covered with a dark blanket could symbolize the rump of a rearing horse about to throw its rider—a third man sitting on their backs.

New York theatergoers spoke in wonder at this skilled stage magician whom the public never knew was black. When he directed Shakespeare's play *The Tempest*, it was as if there was a beach party every night on Prospero's usually forlorn island. When he directed Puccini's opera *La boheme*, it was like new wave French cinema of the 1950s with louche bars in the Latin Quarter of Paris below an outsize film poster of lovers in an extended French kiss.

When young Fatale's parents were badly injured in an auto accident in Harlem, it was a Muslim cleric who first came to help them and who called the police. Don, who was wild with grief, unfairly blamed a Jewish doctor at the hospital for seeming indifference to his parents' serious injuries. By contrast, he was comforted by outsize generosity from this Muslim stranger. When his parents died, this man, who was an imam, helped Don through his grief and made the funeral arrangements. This support led the rising star director to reconsider his life, convert—or revert—to Islam, give up show business, and return to chemistry as an academic.

At Norse Hoven University he rose quickly among the professors to become chair of his department.

At BCU Ace Ferrari appreciated how useful this talented star chemist with the second string to his bow could be. They had met, apparently by chance, over coffee and bagels in the departure hall of the Norse Hoven Railroad Station with its vaulted ceiling and high clerestory windows. Don was waiting for a delayed Amtrak train to Boston.

A newspaper headline about the Middle East had stirred them into heated agreement against US support for Israel and what they both saw as double standards in America's treatment of the Palestinian people. Their liberal beliefs were outraged by the presence of western troops in Saudi Arabia and various military and economic attacks on Iraq.

What Ferrari wanted was Fatale's support for his local, informal Oryx Party based at BCU.

"We are the Arabian Oryx, the elegant antelope of the majestic desert. It embodies the stamina and courage it takes men and animals to survive in the unforgiving desert of Arabia. We are one of many local organizations across the

United States that support and nourish organizations like Hezbollah and Hamas and other movements opposed to Israel. We work to consolidate Muslim feeling and to help Hezbollah and Hamas financially to give their young supporters opportunities stateside."

Knowing Fatale had been a star director, Ferrari had learned his own speech of welcome. He shaped his key phrases skillfully. He got Fatale to tell him what he knew about Hezbollah and Hamas. Fatale knew they were both militant movements against Israel in the Middle East— Hezbollah to get Israel out of Lebanon in the civil war there and Hamas to support the Palestinian people in their double struggle against Israeli occupation and western interference there by the US and France.

Fatale felt drawn toward Ferrari, in part because he was aware of the drift of some young Muslims towards a revived global Islam. Fatale understood that Ferrari wanted him to join the Oryx Party, partly because he was at a neighboring university and thus could broaden party recruitment of young men.

Confident that his enticing words would fall on receptive ears, Ferrari played on Fatale's natural human sympathy as he presented Hamas as a benign social welfare movement:

"Hamas funds education and has built Islamic charities, libraries, mosques and education centers for women. They also build nurseries and kindergartens and supervize religious schools that provide free meals to children. People made homeless by warfare and refugees from Israel's illegal occupation can claim financial and technical assistance from Hamas."

Ferrari was content to leave it there for the moment.

First came a flashing white light, then utter blackness made more disturbing by the contrast. Then he saw a flashing white light again.

For seconds, Modest simply did not know where he was. When he started, he upset his artist's easel. Then his eyesight came back, but hazy. He sat down on the bed. When his mother called him for dinner, he did not hear her. When she came upstairs to see why he was not down, he was pale as a sheet.

"Mama, my eyes are blurry."

Anna had a premonition. She called a neighbor who drove them both to the hospital of the great Milhous College.

With just a cursory glance and before he dilated Modest's eyes, specialist Dr. Chicago guessed what was happening. For Anna, the wait while Modest's eyes dilated, her determination to keep calm, and her awful premonition, were the most uncomfortable things she had ever had to endure. Then came bad news.

"Modest, you're having what we call a detachment. You're very short-sighted. This is because your eyes are long, so long that the retina, the screen, has gotten overstretched. It's pulled too thin. It's beginning to split. We can try and save it. We're going to use laser surgery. That means we don't need to sedate you, cut into the eye."

It had been so sudden. Modest was shaken. Anna was agitated.

Next day, down what seemed innumerable corridors, mother and son went hand in hand until Modest, by himself, entered a room with so much bulging equipment, dark gray and globular, that, in a moment of curious evasion, he fancied he was in a storage depot for a *Star Wars* movie.

He sat bolt upright at a movable desk, then forward with his chin resting on, and into, some metal cage for his face.

As he shone a light into Modest's eyes, one after the other, while holding a magnifying glass, Dr. Chicago gave him directions—"Look up, look down, look left, look right, now upper right, upper left, lower left, lower right."

Each direction made Modest more nervous. Now Dr. Chicago wanted him to take a firm grip, to stay perfectly still. "Resta immobile," he muttered. The outlandish nose of one of the ungainly machines pressed its snout close to Modest's eye and gave out a minute puff of air. All Modest remembered later was blackness interspersed with bright light flashing, not white but yellow. Then his eye seemed to see everything confused and green. There were whining noises and mighty individual clicks. He sensed burning but could not be sure if that was true or just his terror.

Afterwards Dr. Chicago said, "Modest needs to rest now and come back for a check up next week."

Anna wanted to make Groznyy understand how serious was Modest's new eye crisis on top of his basic eye condition. She did not want Groznyy to swat the issues aside after their evening meal when he was tired. So she and Modest went to see Groznyy during his working day. He was in a meeting. There was nothing else to do but wait in the provost's outer office.

Neither of the two pairs of people there wanted to discuss their problems in front of the others who were strangers. So, Anna and Modest, and Ace Ferrari, dean of psychology, and his nephew, Saleem, a dark young man with a face showing scars from some lab accident, sat in moody silence. Saleem had come for the provost's signature on some visa application.

Scanning the forms, secretary Bee Flute reflected that the dean preferred Italian-sounding names for his visiting nephews, exotic as suited their tanned complexions. Bee sensed the names had been carefully chosen to seem glamorous rather than threatening—something an obvious Arabic name might be.

As they looked round the office, the visitors settled on a reproduction of a painting behind Bee's desk: *The Tower of Babel* by Pieter Bruegel the Elder.

71

It reminded Anna of the Colosseum in Rome, which she had visited on a school trip when she was a teenager. Modest read her thoughts and said, "That's because of all the columns and arches in the tower. That's the way the Romans built large buildings."

Ace Ferrari joined in to enlighten his nephew.

"Bruegel, who came from the Netherlands, was playing on the story in the Bible about the high tower men built to reach the heavens as if to challenge God. Renaissance men also saw the Tower as a symbol of the turmoil between the Roman Catholic Church with services in Latin and the Protestant Lutheran religion of the Netherlands with services in local languages."

The nephew was not interested. He simply said, "You can tell it's all falling apart."

Modest remembered that remark later.

"That's the point. God destroyed the tower because of men's presumption, scattering them and making them speak different languages so that they were now divided and could never unite against him," said his uncle.

Modest still had his artist's inner eagle eye. He went up close to inspect the painting.

"When you first look at it, the Tower appears to be a series of stable pillars. But, when you look more closely, none of the layers is horizontal. Instead, the Tower is built as a spiral that tilts—like the leaning Tower of Pisa. The arches meant to support the Tower are starting to crumble."

"The young guy is right," said Saleem. "Look, the foundation and bottom layers of the Tower have not been completed but the workers have started on the higher levels. It's bound to fall."

"But do you get the implications?" asked Ace Ferrari. "Is it society itself that is unsound? We won't even talk about what the Twin Towers represent in Manhattan."

Modest imagined the dean casting a warning glance to his

nephew. He was still peering at the picture as best he could. So, the dean saw the tower as a symbol of modern society with its anarchy ready to burst and destroy it. Through the conversation, Anna had been racking her brain for some memory. Then it came to her. Once when her oldest brother was explaining Tarot cards, he had said, "The Tower signifies destruction."

Bee said nothing but resolved to replace the painting with something more American: the Twin Towers of the World Trade Center.

"Well," she thought, "they're like the Rock of Gibraltar: indestructible."

Inside his polluted ivory tower, Cesare Groznyy was beside himself with fury. The princess's spurious back-dated will had worked in Benny's favor just as Benny and the princess had calculated.

"I don't know how they did it without rousing our suspicions," Larry Dawdler confessed. "But they did. The only way it could be undone would be if you found the princess still alive somewhere. But since you told the police she was dead when you recognized the body from the East River, you can't undo that without retracting your original identification. That would open you up to more questions."

Groznyy had been caught off guard in someone else's trap. He could not bear the thought that he had been duped or, worse, that he had duped himself. His default reaction was to parody Benny throwing his hands up like Al Jolson singing "Mammy": "'I am a queen and my life is a scream.' My queen, your queen, my grandmother's queen."

When Larry had left and Groznyy had heard and digested the latest news about Modest's deteriorating eyesight, he was aghast and blamed Anna.

"You come from peasant stock but without peasant strength. I took a risk with you. Long tall glass of water! You've given me an infirmity."

Anna heard no words of comfort, no thought for their son with needs that must surely grow—just blame, blame, blame.

The following week, Dr. Chicago, usually expert in controlling his reactions to difficult medical problems, was excited when Modest came in for his check-up: "It's worked. The laser surgery worked. As far as we can tell now, the retina is firm in place."

"Does my condition have a name?" asked Modest.

"Sure: pathological myopia. It means you are so short-sighted that your eyes have other problems besides you only seeing things close up. There are some 'dos' and 'don'ts,'" added Dr. Chicago before advising against contact sports, bumping the head, and so on.

"What does he plan after college?" he asked Anna.

"Art school. He's good at drawing," answered Anna.

From Dr. Chicago's noncommittal expression, mother and son guessed that Modest's career options might be more limited.

Now that Dean Ace Ferrari had introduced several nephews to BCU and NHU, chair of chemistry Don Fatale guessed his own second purpose in the Oryx Party: not to teach explosives to such recruits but to provide a cover of legitimacy for their presence as graduate students in chemistry.

Although he was swept along by Ferrari's powers of persuasion, Fatale knew when he was being used as Ferrari insinuated increasingly more rabid anti-Jewish propaganda into his ear. Engrossed in the various papers and articles Ferrari supplied him, Fatale began to see the darker side of Hamas, how its military wing engaged in covert activities, such as gathering intelligence on potential targets, procuring weapons, and carrying out military attacks. He read a press cutting in Ferrari's box file at his house:

Hezbollah has turned into a paramilitary organization. It is reputed to have been among the first Islamic resistance groups in the Middle East to use such tactics as suicide bombing, assassination, and capturing foreign soldiers. It uses missiles such as Katyusha and other rocket launchers and detonations of explosive charges.

"You cannot say you are surprised," said Ferrari. "The aim of Hezbollah and Hamas and their supporters overseas, like us, is the elimination of Israel."

Recalling one of his successful Broadway shows with its potent symbol of the two men and their blanket as a rearing horse and the third man as the rider being thrown off, Fatale wondered if he was becoming the frightened horse or the rider dashed to the ground. He thought that Muslims from Africa and Asia would tolerate him as a convert while he was useful to them. He guessed that Dean Ace Ferrari would make more demands.

It was the unguarded photo that did it. Anna picked up a stray photo of a young preppy-looking guy with unruly straight hair, a photo lying on the floor in the hall. At first she thought it was Modest. She recognized him and she did not recognise him. No: Modest's hair had always been curly, like hers. Who could this be?

She did not hear Groznyy close his study door.

However, Anna had a suspicion.

She was on cordial terms with Larry Dawdler. She knew he respected her quiet dignity. The fact that he phoned the day after she found the photo and asked to see her when Groznyy was away in Manhattan told her that this would not be a social visit. When she poured out his coffee, Larry stopped twisting his hands. When he spoke, it was like the dam bursting on the reservoir by White Water Avenue. Nothing could stop him.

"Anna Stasinova, the fact is that Cesare asked me to speak to you. He's too embarrassed to come clean himself."

Anna felt that her heart had missed a beat. She had a sense of something thudding inside her. She said nothing but her eyes opened wide as they did when something unexpected was about to be sprung on her.

"You know that sometimes Cesare has strayed. He gets a lot of flattery from young women who see him through star-struck eyes."

Larry wanted some encouragement to go on. Anna said nothing but he took her silence as a signal to continue.

"Well, the fact is that one of these young women—her name is Esther Vashti—they were together—met in secret—and they've had a child."

"A little boy or a girl?"

"A boy. Not so little. He's a teenager."

This was a double shock. Anna wanted to vomit. Not months but years of Groznyy not lying as he frequently did, not being economical with the truth as he always was, but shutting not just her but also his second son out of his life. Then a fear struck her. Would Groznyy consider this second son his true heir? Was she wrong?

"There's no mistake, no doubt?"

"No, the fact is—and Cesare admits it—he got carried away. He wrote this Esther some letters. She kept them. Very safely. The fact is they're with her brother who is a lawyer."

"Is she trying to blackmail him?"

"No."

"But Cesare knows he has to take care of his son, financially?"

Anna took Larry's silence as assent. She felt the thud-thud-thudding was turning into a pound-pound-pounding. She gripped her coffee cup tighter and upset it over the carpet.

"Here, let me take care of this," said Larry. He bent down,

took the paper napkin and the handkerchief in his pocket and wiped her clothes. Then he began to mop up the coffee table. While she sat frozen, he went into the ultra-bright kitchen, found cloths on the side of the sink, and came back with them. He started scrubbing the coffee stain on the carpet.

Anna was immobile but tears were streaming down her face.

"I'm in no position to complain. I knew he didn't care for me. He wanted a wife from a Russian family to have his son. He divorced his first wife because she couldn't have children. I wanted to get away from my family. My brothers expected me to cook and clean for them. I don't mean they were lazy. Far from it. They worked all hours in my father's barbershop on a grubby side street in Midtown Manhattan. All hours. They thought this was the American way. Then they had the weary commute back to Brooklyn. I thought that life with Cesare would be an improvement."

"And?"

"Well, socially, on the surface. But while my brothers were trapped in toil, Cesare was driven by his ambition. No, that's not right. By his inner demons. People who hate him—not dislike or fear—hate—say he's a devil. But he is consumed with devils inside him. They drive him at top speed. Then in the midst of this mayhem, I have this immense joy: Modest. He makes everything worthwhile."

Larry thought the shock was pulverizing Anna's emotions. Inside her, she was thinking of how best to protect Modest and his inheritance. Would Groznyy turn her out like he had his first wife?

"Anna Stasinova—there's more. Esther told Cesare that their son has serious eye problems. He was born with cataracts. She and her family wanted him raised in care away from here, and Cesare agreed."

Immediately, Anna's heart went out to the tender little

boy. Yet she realized that, with this disabled child, Esther Vashti would never be a threat to her miserable marriage. So, Larry's second news helped steady her.

What a coward Groznyy was. She knew he would rant and rave, making fate and chance the cause of his misfortunes. But, inwardly, he would be sapped, feeling he could never get the heir he wanted.

When Anna's friend, Dr. Squires, heard the story later he thought, but did not say, that the dark place where the vicious Groznyy had fathered his sons upon dear Anna and this Esther had cost both sons their eyesight.

Anna's determination to put Modest's interests first gave her even more perspective. She could withstand Groznyy's tantrums better than before. It was as if she was an outsider looking in on her marriage through a half-open door. Whereas it seemed Groznyy was in charge at home, it was she who had the better inner freedom. This cushioned the shocks. Being thought a mouse was better camouflage than if she had actually been invisible. She was a survivor for her son's sake, if not her own.

Anna knew that Modest would fully understand the professional and emotional implications of his foreshortened eyesight, how it was curtailing his career options. He did not know what to do with his life. After graduating from college, Modest found work not as an artist—not even a commercial designer or as a worker in the haulage business owned by Larry Dawdler that was his usual job in the summer vacation. Instead, once Modest had graduated, he worked as a clerk moving from one temp job to another.

DISCONTENT AND ITS CIVILIZATIONS

When Groznyy went into his office one fine day, he overheard Bee Flute in the outer office on the phone to Lorraine Boe, head of Human Resources. They were discussing the mammoth task Groznyy faced of overhauling individual departments at BCU and raising their academic standards.

"College leaders trying to restructure departments get burned out," said Bee. "There are all the arguments, plus you're working in a disturbing situation. And often it's all for nothing—like finding a new route to purgatory."

Groznyy wanted to explode. What stopped him was a sense that Bee and Lorraine knew things he did not. Bee Flute had all the sagacity of a cheerful Rhode Islander who had served seven previous provosts. And she had all the loyalty of Juliet's nurse: superficial support while the wind was favorable and until the next provost appeared on the horizon.

There it was on top of his desk, a curt letter from President Franklin Miller. On the surface it seemed routine but it carried an unspoken threat:

Dear Mr. Provost,

Please describe your academic priorities for the next four years and provide me with your proposals for administrative restructuring, specifically for drawing dwarf departments together into divisions, combining secretarial talents into pools, plus your plans to pare down secretarial salaries.

Also, please reply to the delightful complaint letter (enclosed), on the charming matter of Schlossberg *pere* at issue with Mordred Stickleman, professor in the History Department.

When he read Miller's letter, Groznyy's envy and resentment surfaced. It flooded his face when he read the impeccably typed grievance letter from Schlossberg *pere*, originally sent to the president:

Dear President Miller,
How long can Babel City University support such a bunch of low-grade losers as you have in your substandard History Department without provoking the parents who pay your fees? Where, oh, where is that crucial academic quality: excellence?

Freia, my once-joyful daughter, is a junior at BCU working towards a major in Liberal Arts before starting a career as a fashion editor in Manhattan. She recently received an astonishing B double minus for the inadequate course in American history. Thus she has dropped her overall average grades—or rather the paltry history professor, one Mordred Stickleman, has under-valued her stellar achievement. She was in tears last Friday. I called the History Department for an explanation—pronto.

The phone call was taken by the department secretary who declined to tell me her full name—only Claire. I later discovered that her full name is Claire Rollinsky. She refused point blank to put me through to Professor Stickleman, saying he was out of the office at the dentist for root-canal treatment. Then, Claire-With-No-Last-Name proceeded to justify your History Department's deplorable standards.

She opined that Freia's paper on financial strategy among robber barons lacked focus; that it concentrated too much on the sex lives of the robber barons and not enough on their teams of salaried managers. Also that Freia had failed to point out the parallels between the organization of large corporations and the Union Army in the Civil War.

With a copy of Freia's paper in front of me, it is all too easy to dispose of these malapert remarks—which La Rollinsky should not be making anyway. Freia has written two concise paragraphs on Civil War companies and another four paragraphs on creeping bureaucracies. I told Ms. Rollinsky that she did not know either the paper or her history.

At this point the previously indisposed Professor Stickleman suddenly picked up the phone from his own, separate extension. He had been listening in all along, lurking like a rat caught in a trap. He proceeded to berate me, accusing me of a sexist attack on Claire Rollinsky in words more appropriate to a construction site than graced academia.

What can we make of your fabled presidential promise of a new age of learning? How can I comfort my alpha-plus little girl?

I await your reply and the university's reconsidered grades.

Yours, in fury,

Simon Schlossberg.

Groznyy knew it was he who was the trapped rat. If he agreed with the parent, he would be letting down the university, perhaps paving the way for a lawsuit and horrible publicity. If he defended Mordred Stickleman, he would be betraying his own unimpeachable high standards. While he could have gladly sent Professor Stickleman off to Mam'zelle Guillotine, he knew he had to defend the university and sidetrack the parent.

"There is one compensation," said Bee, reading his mind with her usual insight. "Everyone in this scenario is Jewish—father and daughter, professor and secretary. Whatever you decide, there's no question of anyone saying by your favoring one party over another that you're being anti-Semitic."

She continued.

"Funny man, Professor Stickleman: I remember what Pauline, his second wife, told me at Lorraine's party Christmas before last. Just before they became an item, he had come home after seeing an off-Broadway production of

Brecht's *The Caucasian Chalk Circle*. He said, to her astonishment, 'I'm a Marxist now!'"

"That figures. Bertolt Brecht was a morally slippery, hard-line Marxist bore."

"Pauline went on to say at Lo's party, 'Half of *Galileo* at a student reading, followed by a morsel of *Mother Courage* in a TV documentary and he was suddenly a Marxist!' These professors are all alike. Like bankers, they make up their rules as they go along."

Cheered by Bee's sarcasm, Groznyy responded to the president's order in a standard way. He handed the letter to an assistant provost, Edie Fixit, a timid soul regarded by the professors as only a notch above a secretary. But from Groznyy's perspective she had the advantage that, like the other players in this scenario, she too was Jewish. Groznyy approved Edie Fixit's insincere apology with its specious justifications of the grading. However, livid at having to protect Stickleman and irritated by how slowly a young temporary secretary was typing Edie's letter, Groznyy threw a can of Coke at her. He shoved the temp out of her swivel chair to take over her keyboard himself.

"Dr. G.," began Bee, using this tiny version of his last name to humanize Groznyy to other staff members. She tugged her red toupee into place and said, "This is no way to get the best out of people—especially when we're in a crisis."

Next day Bee hung a placard with homily advice on the wall behind her desk: "Don't lose your temper. Others don't want it, having as much as they can manage with their own."

"Mr. Provost, here's something else," said Bee when he came in. "It might help and it might not—but only if you stay calm. I've labeled the file 'Leningrad.'"

As he read the file, Groznyy's face lit up with the pleasure of righteous indignation. The memo had given him a lifeline in his private war with Stickleman. And it allowed Groznyy to reflect on how he could torture Stickleman even if he had to save his callow hide.

Mordred Stickleman liked to think he always trod the high ground of moral superiority. So he could not fathom why he should always feel nervous meeting the dreadful Groznyy. After all, they were from the same generation, had graduated from the same class at NYU. In their student days, they had been friendly rivals as street traders, he with academic books, Groznyy with pretzels, soft drinks, and soft porn. But waiting for Groznyy in the provost's outer office, Stickleman was visibly nervous. Not only had Groznyy risen higher while developing a business portfolio that included shares in a construction company, in a copy writing business, and in some hell-on-earth retirement home, but he also held Mordred's fate in his hands. Worse, Stickleman knew that Groznyy would play with him and his emotions like a cat with a mouse.

He hated the way Groznyy deliberately parodied a James Bond villain, sitting at ease in an enfolding armchair in order to ratchet up the tension for his victims. All that was missing was a white cat on his lap. Yet even Stickleman had not reckoned that Groznyy would use background radio music to add extra menace.

Dr. Squires had advised Anna that it might calm Groznyy and help stabilize his erratic moods if, in his office, he had a radio turned on low and tuned into a classical music station. To her surprise, Groznyy agreed to this.

"Sit down, Mordred, my dear fellow," was how Groznyy opened the interview with the detested professor of economic history. "Do you recognize this?" he asked about the music, knowing that Stickleman would not know.

"It's *Pictures at an Exhibition* by Mussorgsky in one of the orchestral versions. My dear son, Modest, is named after

Mussorgsky and one of Tchaikovsky's brothers. Let's hear it better."

Groznyy raised the volume.

"As you know, the score captures the essence of paintings by Mussorgsky's late friend, Hartmann, in musical character sketches."

Stickleman wanted to save his skin. But having to spar with Groznyy on musical appreciation was beyond him. He was in the wrong over the Schlossberg matter. He knew it. As he heard the music for the painting of a Gnome, which Groznyy kindly identified for him, he knew he was being parodied.

"The Gnome is a nutcracker; he breaks nuts.

"This next is the Old Castle—just like us at little BCU—steeped in tradition, somnolent, misty, fading from view because its very graininess degrades it as it fades."

Groznyy continued, using individual sections to compare and contrast Mussorgsky's magical music with Mordred's political misery.

"You wanted to discuss departmental business?"

The music took a playful, youthful turn.

"Now we come to it: the lovely Freia, on the cusp of adulthood, seeking knowledge for her journey through life. Yes, she must be like one of Mussorgsky's Unhatched Chicks, bursting out of her shell.

"Your secretary, perhaps thinking of her own experience, thinks Freia is too interested in people's sex lives. Her father thinks Ms. Rollinsky should be more aware of the managers of the robber barons. What do you say?"

Stickleman held his peace.

"More on Ms. Rollinsky—or should it be Rollover?—later."

Groznyy continued.

"Not the most famous music but the most bizarre subject: the Hut on Fowl's Legs. That is the lair of the flying witch,

Baba Yar. No witches in New England now. But it's not some phantom. It's a clock in the shape of a hut on fowl's legs. We are subject to time remorseless."

This startled Stickleman: Groznyy was describing the clock in the corner of the room.

The sky outside the huge eighteenth-century-style windows darkened as the heavens opened for a brief shower.

"Ah! The Great Gate of Kiev—triumphal entrance to an immortal city! Are you coming in or staying out?"

Just as Groznyy thought he had him, there was an unwanted interruption. For, chanted outside his window, he heard a damnable pop song—or snatches of it. They were singing the refrain from "Hit the Road, Jack." And they followed it by misquoting the final words from "Twenty-four Hours from Tulsa": "You will never, never get back here again."

The prank was childish but Groznyy was beside himself. Stickleman thought he was off the hook of impalement. Then Groznyy's eyes lit up.

"What do you say? That old cliché of Soviet teachers to children who have misbehaved? 'Lenin would never do that.' No, Lenin would never have done that, not even in the city named after him, Leningrad."

Stickleman winced.

"Last summer vacation you led a party of students to the USSR, is that right? Our students, some students from Milhous College and NHU, and a few high school students from Norse Hoven? Right?"

"Yes."

"And you visited Moscow and Leningrad?"

"And Smolensk and Minsk."

"But you started your tour in Leningrad? Right?"

"Right."

"And for one poor little girl, Pearl Ruckus, the tour ended there. Right?"

"Yes, she had been sick with stomach pains. It was

appendicitis. It wasn't diagnosed immediately. Her appendix burst and she got peritonitis."

"Very nasty. So, what did you do?"

"Pearl was hospitalized straightaway."

"And how did you look after poor Pearl?"

"Our insurance provided for medical cover."

"And what did you do, out of charity—Christian or Jewish? Forget the perils of Pauline, your second wife, and concentrate on the perilous situation of poor little Pearl. I hear she's a darn nice girl."

"I was in a difficult situation. I was responsible for everyone else in our party of twenty-five people—students and staff. I had to take care of them."

"By going ahead with the rest of the tour and leaving the poor girl stranded in a dirty Leningrad hospital—a place like the foul cloacae of a Russian eagle. There were bandages thrown on the floor, the floor itself left spattered with god-knows whose blood, and the whole place like the inside of a rotten cadaver. You weren't the only adult but you left her alone, to die alone."

"She didn't die. There were other adults in our party but they couldn't take charge. One was a high school teacher. The other was our departmental secretary. It wasn't their responsibility, their business."

"And your business was your pretty secretary, Miss Rollinsky. Not move over darling but roll over Rollinsky. And the educational tour? Not Smolensk and the Panorama of the Battle of Borodino, oh no. Sex in Smolensk. Merrymaking in Minsk, oh yes. Not Midnight in Moscow but Metro-sex in Moskva. Who could resist your *jeu d'esprit*? Or should I say *Jew d'esprit* since you were playing away? Who could resist you? Certainly not Claire, the easy rollover, oh no. Your Claire, my Claire, my grandmother's Claire. Never have there been so many nights of passion since Cleopatra seduced Julius Caesar.

"Glossing over the surprise that you have any sort of sex life within marriage or outside it, did it not occur to you that you were not only putting the poor student's life in danger but also the reputation of the university that pays your salary—not to mention possible legal embargoes on our ability to have field trips in future?"

Stickleman was cornered again and this time without an escape hatch. "Reputation?" was the only word that stumbled from his lips.

"Reputation, yes, reputation, fucking reputation!" Groznyy yelled at him. He stood up, came over, and bent his leering head right into his victim's face.

"And how do I know all this? Huh? Because an English patient in the next hospital bed told her folks, who *had* stayed behind to look after her when *she* fell ill. They called the US consulate who phoned her family here. The consulate helped make arrangements for Pearl Ruckus's father to fly to Leningrad and bring his daughter back stateside. And now, oh yes, we have a fucking lawsuit about the university's dereliction of duty!

"But that's all right, provided the sexually repulsive Professor Stickleman could, at long last, get his leg over bimbo de jour Rollover Rollinsky, while the university pays for the privilege, oh yes. You, the Opposition Party! Don't make me laugh! You, who will never enter the great Gate of Kiev, because, when it comes to research, you haven't the balls to do even so small a thing as raise your little finger. Get out of my office. You're finished here."

Groznyy tugged at Stickleman's chair. Stickleman scuttled to the door but not so fast that he missed the parting shot, "Why did Mark Antony marry Cleopatra? Not to fuck her! Don't be silly. Oh no: to stop the spread of communism!"

Stickleman turned round. Groznyy deliberately threw away his next line: "Just a little bit of history repeating."

Then he belched and broke wind.

Stickleman heard Groznyy's final snort of derision as he skittered down the corridor and for long afterwards in his nightmares.

But there was nothing Groznyy could do to undo the mess Stickleman had made for him to clean up without adverse publicity for little BCU. Bee told her husband about it later. He said, "The lawsuit will drag on way after the characters have left the scene."

But the final sting in the tail of the unsavory episode belonged to Stickleman. The day after his interview with Groznyy he bent down in the entrance hall to retie a shoelace. On the stone floor he saw a scuffed sheet of drawing paper.

When he picked it up and smoothed it out, he saw it was a cartoon drawing of Groznyy addressing his Kitchen Cabinet in a Monday morning breakfast harangue. Groznyy himself looked like a wolf with snake's eyes. There were his staff trying to suppress their yawns: roly-poly Lorraine Boe as a sheep in sheep's clothing; world-weary Larry Dawdler with a glazed stare; Bee Flute fiddling with two askew toupees; and assorted office staff presented as screeching birds in a not very nice cage. The style was pop art satire. The best joke was the caption bubbling out of Bee's opulent lips. It was the title of a song by rock group Queen: "I Want to Break Free."

But who was the artist?

With savage inner satisfaction, Stickleman took it back to his beloved and they pondered how to use it. Claire Rollinsky knew. For implied future favors she passed the anonymous cartoon to a history major student who wrote for the students' weekly paper, *Student Babble On*. When the next issue came out, the drawing was all over campus and so was the unanswered question: "Who Has Done This?"

Larry Dawdler pacified Groznyy by persuading the

supreme narcissist that no publicity was bad publicity because it got everyone talking about you. Though the source of the widespread merriment remained unknown, the merriment was far from innocent.

Hence the scene was set for the controversies inherent in the clash of ambitions. On one side, self-seeking professors who wanted business as usual even when their own decline and fall was staring them in the face. On the other the self-seeking president and provost. One was intent on reward by position; the other intent on further reward by conspicuous wealth.

President Franklin Miller was concerned by the rising tide of antipathy to Groznyy and the way ripples of discontent tarnished his own reputation. Groznyy realized that the earlier candor between them was now lukewarm, chilled by winds of lasting coldness. Indeed, Groznyy knew he was in big trouble. His rages to deans and administrative staff, his successive denials of tenure to complacent junior professors—all had the opposite effect from what he had expected. Instead of raising his profile as a pioneer academic, his behavior had made him the object of distrust. He was an isolated figure. Groznyy knew Miller would sacrifice him in a trice to save his own hide.

With a heavy heart Groznyy met the president by the monument surmounting Great Rock away from BCU because no one would be there. To avoid being seen, the president traveled there by taxi and was waiting for Groznyy.

"We can't have this any longer," Miller told him. "Instead of imposing higher academic standards on BCU, your brutal tactics have caused uproar and destabilized everything a university depends on–steadiness and freedom of academic thought. You have outsize talents but nothing is for the common good—your polished charm when it suits you, your excessive praise, cataclysmic rages, and, finally, malicious putdowns. Everything must emanate from you and everyone is expected to pay court."

Miller continued.

"There's the unfortunate way you cajoled Bedfellow Burns out of his house. Then there's the even more unfortunate way Bedfellow Burns's mother—whom you had made homeless—died of exposure. You can excuse yourself, wrap it up with words, but people blame you. There was your calculated humiliation of your dangerous enemy, the scurvy Stickleman. When your task was to get the university off the hooks of disgrace he had forged, all you did was deepen his hatred without being able to kill him off.

"The professors' ripples of discontent have infected the trustees. You have to go. I don't want headlines now. We will wait until the calm period—the Christmas inter-session. Then, you will leave without brass fanfare—or whimper—in order to complete your never-started magnum opus on Nietzsche."

A dark lock of hair no longer jet-black but with threads of gray clung to Groznyy's forehead. Miller thought he looked like a trapped animal.

"Give me one more chance," was a plea that would never have fallen from the lips of Ivan the Terrible of Russia and it did not fall from the lips of little Nemo Groznyy. Groznyy was nothing if not a fighter. He had a plan that would raise the status of this little university with its rag-tag professors.

"Before you decide, let me show you something."

Miller said nothing when he got into Groznyy's car. The likelihood of summary execution never left them. They drove down the winding hill from Great Rock to the twin cities below, through a dark thicket of bushes and trees that seemed never to have been touched by the sun.

Groznyy said, "This little wood reminds me that in Russia

all around us there are foreign parts—chuzoi. These are dangerous. In cottages and dachas, there are spirits—domovoi—who look after families inside."

"You like the reassurance of domovoi? Tell me about your domovoi."

This was his opportunity. Groznyy had long thought the science departments at BCU should be run more economically. He would show Miller what should be their domovoi. He had a scheme that would harness neighboring Norse Hoven University's one strength to back him up—its medical school—and add the prestige of Milhous College, the great Ivy League institution, to the mix.

"We have to go to our small neighbor, Norse Hoven University. I know what you think. But although NHU may be broke, it's far from poor."

Once in the blue-collar suburbs, they parked the car on a leafy street outside NHU. As they criss-crossed a courtyard with russet-stone Gothic buildings, Miller noted a tic fluttering under Groznyy's face as he spoke.

"NHU is trying to become a better teaching and research university. Like BCU, it's within striking distance of New York. NHU was originally named Lazarus College to symbolize uniting Jewish and Christian values The Jewish name Lazarus was also the name of the first man Jesus raised from the dead. But after World War II, Lazarus College was in decline. There was the threat of us—Babel City University—in affluent suburbs closer to the Sound and a competitor for students."

Groznyy guessed that it would be better to let the president draw breath before producing the rabbit out of his magician's hat.

"I remember," said Miller. "It was one of the few medical schools that did not impose a secret quota on Jewish students. Some people thought that this was why the American Medical Association was reluctant to accredit it."

Groznyy knew he had to lead Miller on as if Miller himself had come up with the idea that Groznyy was about to put to him.

"A committee of prominent New York rabbis was looking for a campus on which to found a secular university," Groznyy added tentatively.

The two men entered an odd round building.

"There's no arts-and-sciences building here as such," said Miller, waving his cane at the main entrance. "The dean's office has been incorporated in this preposterous Science Building. It aims for striking modernism. But its glass facade is paltry—a galumphing edifice."

"That's only the outside," added Groznyy. "Inside, see, it's decorated with the ugliest tiles you've ever seen—blue, beige, and sepia—like a soiled lavatory in a rundown railroad station."

He continued.

"So, what did the trustees of Lazarus College do? They told the rabbis they would give them the campus and the charter of their college with the proviso that they would improve the School of Medicine. Location *was* everything. The rabbis were excited by the opportunity to secure this great site near New York, the city with the premier Jewish community in the world. The trustees of Lazarus and the rabbis agreed to rename the college Norse Hoven University—a neutral name with no religious connotation."

As they left the Science Building, Franklin Miller, still swinging his cane, took the high road of moral principle.

"They got good press. This Jewish-sponsored university was to be without quotas and open to all, regardless of race, color, or creed. There was a sound moral purpose—merging the honorable Hebraic tradition in which culture is a universal birthright and the equally honorable American aim of supporting democracy by widening educational opportunities."

Groznyy wanted to stay focused on his plan for his own survival.

"Its continued revival depends on merging its hospital and medical research facilities into a consortium with other local colleges, including us—Babel City University—and Milhous College."

Miller took the bait.

"We have a mission here. The various colleges in Norse Hoven and Babel City can only compete with the best medical and scientific communities across America if they combine to create a consortium that will include a new joint science park."

"At last, he's got it," thought Groznyy triumphantly.

"This is where you take the lead. From time to time, Milhous College makes token gestures to reach out to other colleges in the county. But these are empty declarations."

Miller let Groznyy lead him.

"Milhous cannot take official control of your proposed consortium. That would be like the whale swallowing Jonah. They need us."

Groznyy applied flattery with a trowel.

"They need you as president to run the show. You can move BCU into the top rank of US universities. That will be your legacy."

Miller agreed.

After negotiations and due processes, the three colleges decided to join resources to create a science consortium and a science park. After an agreeable joint press statement, the unpopular Groznyy, still provost but even now under notice from Miller that he might be forced out, had to fix the nuts and bolts of academic cohesion. He had to make the consortium work, get funds flowing, and bind the different elements together: professors and scientists, labs and hospital units. Then, he would be safe. Luckily, Larry

Dawdler and a new trustee, Veronica Veneer, head of an African American construction company, had the resources to assemble the building blocks.

Advised by Dawdler on how important it was to run science labs and medical units with a uniform approach to income and costs, Groznyy interviewed one Oliver Swindle of Scientific Sticklers. Dawdler had a substantial business interest in this company.

Swindle was a dapper dandy, a repressed gay glad to look older than his years so that no one would suspect him of sexual feelings. He was a drier stick than any a scoutmaster put on a campfire.

"The teams involved in research at our trio of colleges raise funds from various sources—corporate, government, and academic," said Groznyy. "The funds pay for equipment, materials, and salaries. Milhous, NHU, and we at BCU charge our departments some of their funds for space, heat, and light, according to the space they occupy."

"Yes, Mr. President. Our argument at Scientific Sticklers is that the only way to apportion costs fairly is not by space but by precise measurement of energy use—lab by lab, medical unit by medical unit."

Hence, in the name of better academic accountability, and, not least, to save his own skin, Groznyy persuaded the board of trustees to support a comprehensive costs review by Larry Dawdler's company, Scientific Sticklers, managed by Oliver Swindle.

"He will fill the prissy shoes of a time-and-motion expert to perfection," said Franklin Miller.

Together, president and provost pored over Oliver Swindle's colleague who would investigate the hospital complex. Dolly Drum, now married and using her full new name of Dolly Drum Dong, reminded Groznyy that not long ago she had been one of the students whom he had rescued from Ashley Bedfellow Burns. She used the fragrance of her

Macy's perfume to titillate him although her dress code was standard Manhattan gray cloud.

While Groznyy and Miller were playing houses with the new science consortium, Lorraine Boe faced a shade from the past. There was nothing new in that. It was her lot as head of Human Resources at BCU. But not every day was it going to be in her power to find work for her ex-husband, Brad Gable. She had not seen him since their divorce a few years earlier. He looked older, as she did. But whereas she had taken precautions with her colored, backcombed bouffant hair, her tense girdle and her upholstered cleavage, her floral print blouses, and her skilled makeup, he had let himself go. He was still the dumpy bald man with the bubbly manner.

When he had first courted her, Brad's hands had roamed all over her body. He used to murmur, "Just like a chicken, a succulent roast chicken, all breasts and thighs, just needs stuffing." She had wondered, "Why am I doing this? I could do better." But then she would remember her mom repeating Mae West's throwaway line, something like, "A man may be short, fat, and rapidly balding but if he has fire, women will go for him." And go for him Lorraine did, even though her mom had also warned her that Brad Gable had no career future since all his work was as a security guard. But when, to test her affection, he mentioned that he had Type 1 Diabetes, she melted, like the compassionate soul she was.

Brad and Lo had been blissfully happy when they were first married for he knew how to please her sexually, up and down, front and aft. But his fire went into his true passion—jazz. That passion spent itself increasingly on young ladies who sang the blues, jazz singer hopefuls, "little chantoot-sies," Lo's mom called them. He wanted to be a star-maker. And if they were tempted by his casting-couch eyes, so much the better. So Lorraine faced diminishing returns in sex and companionship although Brad was always a good provider at home. Not every would-be singer was like an over-easy egg in an American diner—ready to be turned over. But tell-tale signs of lipstick on his collar, smudged handkerchiefs, and missing underwear told Lorraine tales she could not ignore and it hurt damn bad.

Their divorce had been amicable. Wherever he went, Brad would send her postcards without any edge, written as cheerfully as if they had been childhood sweethearts who remembered one another affectionately.

Now he was back. Rather than embarrass him, Lorraine helped him over the first ledge of their conversation.

"Don't tell me. You were let go. Your diabetes has been playing up. You need work but not hard work. Well, you've come to the right person. But you knew that anyways. Colleges have their teams of security guards. Here, we're talking dangerous downtown in Norse Hoven. The kids need protecting the moment they step off campus at night. I'll get you a daytime shift to begin with. The pay is less but the main thing is for you to get your strength back first."

"Thank you, Lo."

"You owe me big."

When he smiled, she felt warm as she had not since they broke up.

Brad had always been a reliable worker. Lorraine had fewer worries about taking him on than she would have had about taking on her jailbird brother in Bikers Island, the offshore prison. With regular work, a humble apartment on White Water Avenue that Lorraine found for Brad and that became his new base for scouting out singing hopefuls, Brad was back in business. Then he had heard this new talent sing in a local bar. When she finished the "Trolley Song," he simply said, "Wow!"

96

LOVE HANDLES

It was not love at first sight. It was love at second sight. And for one of them, it would be love forever.

Lorraine Boe was recruiting students and family members at BCU as well as other workers through temp agencies. Would Modest like to earn some extra cash in a project that might open doors for future opportunities?

Indeed, Modest's next temp job promised more than it delivered. He was to take part in an assessment of energy use among science and medical departments in the new consortium of the three universities. The pay was seven dollars an hour.

Modest turned up late and out of breath for the opening meeting in a grubby lecture room. He had mistaken the way in the labyrinthine corridors linking physics to chemistry in Milhous College and got lost.

The balding speaker at the podium was in full flow. A paper circulated round the room for the temps to sign their names.

"Our name is Scientific Sticklers. We're smart movers in irregular research."

The speaker made a noise halfway between a laugh and a cough.

"Like all major universities, Milhous College and the others in the consortium devote considerable resources to medical and scientific research across all sorts of labs.

"But there are flaws: Milhous, Babel City University, and Norse Hoven University's assessment of charges by the university to individual units is simply based on cubic space and a very general determination of the use of heat and light. That's where we come in. We are an enterprising—"

"Not to say finagling," said a young woman sitting next to Modest.

"Excuse me speaking while you're interrupting," barked the moderator.

Modest turned. He saw, illuminated in the dappled sunshine from the windows, a girl with glowing Titian hair and a budding figure.

"Has a way with words, this Oliver Swindle," added the young woman.

"Oliver Swindle? Is that his name?" Modest whispered back.

"Is the pope Catholic?" she replied. "I'm Hermione— Hermione Eterna."

"I'm Modest Groznyy."

She looked him over while he was appreciating her physical charms. Standing five feet, ten inches he weighed 170 pounds. His special physical features were his muscular shoulders and well-defined torso, not to mention his open face, generous smile, and engaging manner.

Oliver Swindle was still in oratorical flight.

"You will have the honor of examining each lab, then of making an inventory of equipment. You will then impose calculations of energy use by applying the company's tables."

By now, the induction room was full. Several temp agencies had assembled workers to be trained over an initial week. After training, teams of twos were to work through labs, studios, and so on, making inventories, clockwise from the entrance of each unit. The calculations that followed were complex, involving measurements of size and energy, then additions for this, subtractions for that, and comparisons with the other.

"Sounds like Byzantine mathematics," said Hermione.

She explained that she had finished college last year with a major in music, specifically piano, and that she was going to start a graduate course in arts administration at the Tisch School in New York the following year.

Both Modest and Hermione had known the world of temp agencies long enough to recognize types of temps: harried young parents; callow youths escaping their new parental obligations; divorcees trying to start over again; mature ladies returning to work after the kids had left home; and, like themselves, college kids learning the American way. However, Modest and Hermione were surprised to see some Arab-looking men among the temps.

At first, the temps said nothing to one another but they found plenty wrong with the energy survey. Modest and Hermione detected flaw upon flaw in the company's energy re-assessments. Over lunch they joined wits with the other temps.

"It's way better than my last temp job," said a young African American.

"Which was?"

"Cutting labels from tops saying 'Made in China' for someone else to switch by sewing designer-brand labels in their place."

"It's a lark," said a woman, nestling her arms in her husband's.

Turning round from the next table, Oliver Swindle swept this aside: "Young woman, our analysis has been approved at the highest echelons of the three universities."

"That's papa, all right," thought Modest.

The little group concentrated on munching its dry sandwiches. It was the old story. They had arrived at Scientific Sticklers with as much meekness as if they had gone to prison. Indeed, that afternoon, the temps performed their functions like prisoners prowling round a jail exercise yard.

Once he felt comfortable with her, Modest told Hermione that he had problems seeing properly—pathological myopia he said. The time he most needed her eyesight to help him was the morning she was away at the dentist. Thus when Modest came to assess a lab by himself, his heart sank. It was a long green corridor so dim that candles might have lit it.

Modest's sight was now so poor that everything seemed dark unless he was outside on a bright but not sunny day. If the sun came out suddenly or he was in a room and someone turned on an overhead fluorescent light, the effect was like a Nazi trooper shining an arc light on an escaping refugee. What colors Modest saw were murky. Reds became browns, blues became indigos, and whites and creams became streaked ochers. It was a world of mottled saffron. He now had double vision. When it was particularly uncontrollable, everything collided with everything else. Stationary objects moved and rippled.

There were objects Modest did recognize—such as microwave cookers and refrigerators, scissors and spoons—and also basic lab equipment—such as test tubes. But others were strange and mysterious to anyone who had left science behind at high school. Their colors were black on gray or cream on white. Their material was translucent glass on opaque glass, or copper on zinc, or aluminum on steel. Their shapes—oval or round, spiky or chunky—mingled and jostled together.

Advised by Supervisor Swindle to take a deep breath and thus avoid a panic attack when a lab overcrowded with equipment might prove too much, in the next lab, Modest did just that. He proceeded methodically, did the calculations, checked them, and did them again.

Modest was surprised to see a scientist's briefcase left open on a stool. When he moved the stool to get nearer the counter, the briefcase fell over. Out fell what Modest thought was a map. He picked it up. But it was not a geography map. It looked like the blueprint for a Boeing plane showing, as far as Modest could tell, the position of the fuel tank outlined in red crayon.

Thinking how odd it was to find such a plan in a

chemistry lab, he wondered what the scientist had to conceal. When he heard the lab door open, he put the map under the briefcase and steadied the stool.

Modest tried to look as if nothing was amiss but he was surprised when Mukhtar Saar, one of the Arab guys from the survey, came in. Mukhtar was a burly fellow with an infectious laugh until a serious thought crossed his face and the smile turned into a menacing look. His eyes rested kindly on Modest whom he saw as a boy with a sympathetic manner and hardly a clue as to what was going on.

"Ollie Swindle sent me to help you. I studied chemistry in grad school."

Modest was relieved.

"Thanks a heap."

Then came a second surprise. Mukhtar and the chemistry researcher, a man with gleaming eyes and a large hooked nose, who had just returned to the lab, clearly knew one another. His face seemed familiar. Mukhtar started working at the other side of the lab in an anti-clockwise direction so that he and Modest would meet in the middle and then review one another's work. First he made a few social comments to the researcher. Then their idle chitchat took a more serious turn.

"Saleem," Mukhtar asked, "are these clocks?"

"Yup, that about sums it up. These clocks can be used like egg timers—and what do you suppose cracks open?" said Saleem. "Humpty Dumpty with his cock at the ready! These remote controls are first-rate for setting off blasts at a distance."

Mukhtar continued to press Saleem.

"So, this explosive is good for this attack; this for another," he continued, referring to what looked to Modest no more than pellets.

Saleem looked up.

"He's a good egg," said Mukhtar to reassure the researcher.

Mukhtar told Modest that he was the nephew of the chair of chemistry and that Saleem was a nephew of the dean of psychology. Then Modest remembered he had seen Saleem in Bee Flute's office with his uncle.

By now the two young men had switched languages and were speaking in what Modest assumed was Arabic. He thought it best to go on working as if he had heard nothing. The dark room and the stupid nature of the task took their toll. Two-and-a-half hours later and Modest was wringing with sweat. He crumpled on a half ledge on a wall outside the entrance.

When Hermione returned to work after lunch, Modest had never been so pleased to see anyone. He hugged her tight. The hug became a tender kiss as their two heads bobbed and weaved together. Their ample tresses got entangled as they embraced on the steps of the Natural History Museum. For there lay their mission that afternoon, calculating the heat and light cost of university livestock.

The curators of museum labs housing insects—stick insects with ravenous jaws and other insect globules—delighted in showing off their charges to the little ersatz scientific team. The insects were neatly compartmentalized as mewling infants, cocky teenagers, breeding parents, and old codgers. Without a care, the insects chomped away at vegetation.

In their stolen bliss, Modest and Hermione were comforted to realize that each was thinking the same as the other: the temps were just like the insects—confined, lacking control of their lives. The competing vices of ambition, distraction, and derision of the two courts of little BCU—the Groznyy Gang and the Opposition Party—were symptomatic of the delusions of self-interested groups of society beyond. They did not then know and could not add the Oryx Party to the mix.

Modest thought he had probably made some mistakes

that morning. Hermione was more than ready to go back to the chemistry lab to help put them right. While they were doing some re-checking, they saw that a computer screen was switched on. Hermione read out what looked like a draft letter:

> From the Advance Brigade of Freedom Fighters:
> If you do not agree to our just demands on behalf of the Palestinian people, our units will proceed against military and civilian targets across the United States. Our brigade comprises a hundred soldiers ready to die in our just cause. This is a message. We could just as easily blow you up.

Modest and Hermione were startled but they did not discuss it there and then in case the Arab scientists suddenly returned and found them there.

In their afternoon break the survey team began asking one another what they liked to do in their leisure time.

When it was Mukhtar's turn, he said, "What do I like to do in my leisure time?" He winked. "Well, my biggest craze used to be killing off American scientists. You know, I really enjoyed it. It turned me on. You can kill them on the street like muggers do with knives and guns. In a lab you can kill them by gassing them. If you have the funds, you can kill them with bombs. There are all sorts of ways."

"Used to be your craze?" asked Hermione provocatively. "Why?"

"Used to be because now my little list would be longer and include Mr. Oliver Swindle and his assistant, Miss Dolly Drum Dong. You wait till you meet her—she's bad news. Then there's the master puppeteer behind Dong and Swindle—the damned provost and his damned survey."

"But why the scientists?"

"Because it was American scientists who made the atomic bomb and later devised and perfected napalm."

General surprise.

Undeterred, Mukhtar became expansive.

"These college professors go on and on about irony, dramatic irony, and the rest. But they never mention the supreme irony of themselves as pawns of the American state or of Jews becoming like the Nazis who oppressed them in the 1930s and then killed them in the 1940s. Now Jews in Israel use the same means against the Palestinians, first marginalizing them and then putting them in what are concentration camps in all but name. And the American people support all this."

"But you can't expect the American people to know where every last nickel and dime of their taxes go," argued Hermione.

"Ignorance is no excuse. It's no justification to say that they don't know where their tax money goes. I expect today's students to be radical. And what did traditional anarchists say a hundred years ago? 'Property is theft, government is tyranny.' So what should be our remedy? 'Anarchy is justice.'"

Afterwards, Hermione said to Modest, "These young Arab guys are fired up against us all right. But they never mention inequalities in Arab societies, wealth versus poverty, or dictators who hang on to power, making it impossible for democratic opposition to make its voice heard or to prepare more representative forms of government."

Two weeks earlier, Modest would have had no interest but when he read a spare flier for an early evening lecture at Milhous College, free and open to all, he knew he had to go. The title was "Why Arabs Dislike US Policies." Modest could not get the plane map and Mukhtar's comments out of his mind.

Just before they went into the lecture room, Hermione

saw a notice board with messages about the Arab–Israeli conflict and America's partiality to Israel. There was a disclaimer at the head of the board:

> Milhous College respects the right of people to express their independent opinions. Those posted below are personal and do not represent any official opinion of Milhous College except for the college's commitment to freedom of speech.

Then Hermione read out two messages.

> In his search for racial purification, Hitler had the right idea but not the right target. It was not the Jews who infected the world with impurity but the Anglo-Saxons. First the British who were arrogant and greedy in the way they overran the globe and brutal and vicious in the way they ruled their colonial subjects even as they claimed to be fighting World War II to free Poland. And then their heirs as world policemen, the Americans who behaved as know-alls while knowing little and understanding less as they brutalized Vietnam with carpet bombing and napalm in the name of spreading democracy. What a mockery!
> Student Union at NHU.

Another message took a wider perspective.

> It's the same story. The Bolsheviks said it and under Stalin went on repeating it. The Chinese Communists said it and under Mao Zedong went on repeating it: "We have to kill millions of people so that millions more people will be happier in future." And what happened? All we can be sure of is that millions of people died. And for what? Were millions happier afterwards? This has been a cry in the name of freedom ever since the French Revolution. In this century two terrible world wars and horrible civil wars in Ireland, Spain, China, and Vietnam. Millions dead. Millions happier?

Survivors pay with their conscience. It eats away at them. This has been the case ever since the protest against American involvement in Vietnam crystallized a growing mood of distrust against conventional deference to the political establishment.

Zenocrate Cohen.

Modest said, "I think she's a Zionist and she works in papa's office."

They went in and sat at the back of the shabby lecture room. Mukhtar was two rows in front.

"Typical of Milhous, isn't it?" said Hermione. "They waste all that money on the silly energy survey while their physical plant is falling apart."

When the talk began, the young loves were somewhat surprised by the seemingly calm exterior of the smartly dressed young speaker with a charming Middle Eastern accent. His said his name was Darius Esen. His initial manner contrasted sharply with his increasingly passionate words. Modest and Hermione were taken aback by his focus on the ever-present Israeli–Palestinian conflict and the angle of his attack.

"It's elementary. Israel allows—no, it encourages—its soldiers to kill tender little children in Palestine while America kills innocent Arabs in their very own countries. And during all their barbaric acts, the American people support their empty-headed president. The American people resist—no, fight against—proper standards of morality. They stand by and allow their taxes to be used to fight the mujahideen. You bet we've got the right to fight back."

Someone in the audience interrupted. He was a man with receding curly hair and a collected manner.

"Isn't all this extreme?"

The charming speaker was ready.

"Anyone who commits murder and anyone who assists the murderer by giving them money or weapons—well, they have taken part in the original crime. They must be punished."

Once again, the discontented man spoke up, this time with more fervor.

"I'll ask you again, isn't this extreme?"

"But it's exactly what the West does. Look at the way the United States behaves towards Iraq and Libya. It uses policies to penalize all the people for the faults of the regime."

The audience was silenced by the authoritative tone of Professor Mordred Stickleman of BCU who had been sitting unnoticed until then.

"My friend, you're fresh out of college. You should be for freedom and liberty—not only the Palestinian people but also the poor people living beside you in Louvre Ville. You're falling into the trap set by the capitalist class. The fundamental truth about oppression is that it succeeds by turning its victims against one another instead of their oppressors."

Then the unknown man with the receding hair started up again.

"You've got it horribly wrong about Israel. You're speaking about a small country surrounded by enemies and almost defenseless in the land God promised his people. The Israelis' birthright to live there is before recorded history. The Israelis suffered two Diasporas, first from the Babylonians under Nebuchadnezzar, then from Imperial Rome under Vespasian and Titus.

"After centuries of hostility when everywhere they traveled governments told them they had no right to live among Christians, they were almost wiped out in Hitler's Holocaust when Germany told them they had no right to live at all.

"And this is the unspeakable horror into which you want to plunge God's chosen people for a third time!

"How can you stand here in a land of born-again Christians, whose forefathers fought for the universal rights of man, and preach your gospel of hate? You don't deserve to breathe the same air as presidents like Lincoln and Roosevelt. And it's Jewish thinkers Marx, Einstein, and Freud whose pioneering ideas changed the way we perceive and interpret the world."

With that, the angry man in the audience got up and upset some of the folding chairs in the lecture room. Turning round at the door, he yelled, "How can you say such things in a democratic country? You are not even worthy of the name of scum."

"The urge to destroy is also a creative urge," Darius Esen shouted back.

Darius thought he had made his point and he also left, but through a back door. The meeting disintegrated. As they left, Hermione asked Mukhtar, "Didn't the angry man at the front have a fair point?"

Mukhtar was calm.

"He would say that, wouldn't he? Americans are just as responsible as Israelis for the crimes Israel commits in Palestine. America bankrolls these crimes and gives Israel weapons. The funds come from taxes paid by the American people. This makes the American people accessories to the establishment of illegal settlements beyond Israel's official borders, and the imprisonment, torture, and killing Israel metes out to the Palestinian people."

Hermione felt deep outrage.

Mukhtar sensed that Modest was more intrigued.

Next day Mukhtar was absent from the survey. The day after, he was back. He thought he recognized a sympathetic audience in Modest and Hermione. He told them how, the day before, he had traveled to Philadelphia on a low-flying aircraft for an interview for a university research job. The interview had been in the airport. His two young co-workers expected him to be enthusiastic about his job prospects. But all he could think about was the flight.

"Imagine. We were so near the skyscrapers in New York. The World Trade Center, why, it looked like two giant tomb-stones for the poor working stiffs—the suckers—trapped in those outsize coffins. And the Statue of Liberty, why, I was so close I felt I could snuff it out with a swipe of my hand."

This alerted Modest, who was becoming obsessed with the plane map. Then it struck him. He said to Hermione later, "I've got it. Whatever they're going to do, there's a bomb. It can't be big—they wouldn't get it on a plane. Security would find it. But if the bomb was in the passenger seats just above the fuel tank, it could set fire to the fuel and destroy the plane in mid-air."

Possessed by his new idea, Modest went on.

"What Mukhtar wants is to harm the United States with bombs that will damage us just as much, perhaps more, psychologically, than the actual physical destruction, and that will be bad enough."

Hermione thought it would take their minds off what was wrong if she played piano for him. She found an empty studio with a piano in Milhous College.

Modest listened in awe at Hermione's piano playing but it meant nothing to him. The scales and arpeggios sounded like cascades, sure enough. But they might just as well have been cascades in a waterfall that he wanted to get out of. Sensing this with Haydn and Chopin, Hermione thought that more popular tunes might please him. She tried Liszt's operatic transcriptions, starting with the quartet from Verdi's *Rigoletto*. Whatever she tried drew a blank until she moved to Liszt's paraphrase of the Liebestod from Wagner's *Tristan und Isolde*. She sensed a sexual pulse running through Modest. Hermione wondered if she should read this hitherto sullen response to her piano playing as an alarm bell as to their future together. But then she knew nothing about jazz and cared less.

The cops were not sure what they would find. First there had been the extraordinary visit of young Modest Groznyy with girlfriend in tow, two tousle-haired youngsters in floppy tops and figure-hugging jeans. Their story had been striking, if incoherent: some half-assed plot to down airliners with bombs already stowed on board. But which airplanes?

When rising police detective Leo Guerra had interviewed the kids, they were so timid and yet so insistent. Their story came out of nowhere. Truth to tell, Detective Guerra and his rookie sidekick, McSweeny, might have dismissed it out of hand. The officers' usual task was drug busting. But this engaging Modest Groznyy was the son of the awesome provost of Babel City University. Leo Guerra sensed that this winning kid, just out of college, had his father's steely determination. He had never been in trouble. And he showed the police respect. University politics did not interest the officers. But they knew better than to ruffle professorial feathers in an Ivy League town.

"Do you think it's true?" McSweeny asked Guerra as they sipped murky coffee after the youngsters had left. "And why didn't you ask young Groznyy if he had talked it over with his father?"

"There's trouble brewing at BCU. I heard it from my wife who used to work in the admissions office there. The provost despises the professors. The professors hate the provost. It's a bad atmosphere—poisonous. Step into any building at BCU. You could cut the atmosphere with a knife."

Despite misgivings, the police obtained a warrant and searched the second floor of the chemistry building. They found nothing out of the ordinary. No maps of any sort. Nothing on the computers.

"Everything looks spick and span," observed McSweeny.

"Yes. I think that's the point. Nothing out of place—in a lab with all sorts of experiments going on at different stages."

When she heard that the case was going nowhere, Hermione said to Modest, "I shouldn't be surprised but I am. My political science professor always told us that criminals and the police need one another—just like both need lawyers. None of them can exist without the other. There certainly was a mutual relationship between anarchists and the police up to the 1920s."

When he found out, Groznyy was furious.

"You cause this unnecessary problem! Don't I have enough to deal with without this, Mr. Smart-Ass Four-Eyes? You should have told me before going to the cops. How do you think this makes us look?"

Modest was not to be deterred.

"These people want to destroy you—not just you but all of us: bomb us to extinction."

"Don't be absurd. Nowhere is more determined to preserve its educational status than this third-rate institution. The professors have an exaggerated sense of their superiority. This illusion infects all of them—the professors, the students, and their families. That's why little BCU will never be a haven for terrorists. And your supposed terrorists—these puny scientists—are themselves like laboratory animals—confined, conditioned, and too terrified to challenge the Pax Americana that supports their lifestyle."

The argument lasted until evening.

The guests were arriving on cue. They expected delicious dishes at the provost's house, courtesy of a top caterer, and accompanied by stellar wines. What they got was crash, bang, wallop.

Offstage but audible they were treated to the continuing blazing row.

"Does Oliver Swindle actually believe what he's doing is truthful? How could all the intelligent professors give in to this King-and-Duke organization as if they're alchemists who've found the philosopher's stone?"

The quarreling got louder. Suddenly it stopped with the unmistakable sound of someone's face being slapped.

When they went downstairs, father and son faced not just the usual cast of characters but also someone whom Groznyy wanted to charm for the sake of his and Larry Dawdler's joint business interests. This was Veronica Veneer, stylish head of the African American construction company named Blackthorn Buildings already involved in creating some new buildings in Science Park and renovating others.

The guests noted a rising weal on Modest's face. No matter how nice he was, he was his father's son, not least in how feisty he could be. When Veronica Veneer made a polite enquiry about the survey his father said, "It's a real success. Our scientists understand we must re-examine our priorities."

Modest disagreed.

"No. That's not right. Our little teams of scavengers are far from welcome in the scientific community. Some large labs with many people respond courteously—because they're used to many people jostling one another. But labs with scientists in research requiring intense concentration regard us at best as inconvenient, and, at worst, as irrelevant.

"There's a funny side to it as well. In the Milhous chemistry building—the one with the glass curtain wall—our boss, dry stick Swindle presented the lab as the academic base of a Nobel Prize winner. He positively salivated at the prospect of meeting this great lady of

Milhous College. He knocked reverentially at the door. When the door opened, a squat man with a shaved head heaved his torso—peeking out of a grubby T-shirt—and barked, 'Vhadya vant?'

"When the dry stick explained, the shaved head barked, 'I'm not gonna do that. You get the fuck outta here!'

"He banged the door shut. Hermione heard a key turn in the lock. I smelled alcohol on Oliver Swindle's breath."

"Did you recognize this man?" asked Groznyy testily.

"Maybe. With my sight, I can never be sure."

Modest did not see his father's eyes narrow and his lips mouth the name "Don Fatale" to Larry Dawdler. He had guessed that this false Hungarian persona must be chemistry chairman Don Fatale of NHU playing a prank on the unsuspecting Swindle to ridicule the scheme.

Outraged, Groznyy took out his not-so-pent-up anger on the chairs of departments who were not at the dinner party and whom he blamed for every problem: "These rabble-rousers skulking in one another's houses. They prepare vicious assaults while they down bourbons and beer. They reek of petit-bourgeois canapés, pickled herrings and onions."

With that, Groznyy jabbed the table with his expensive pen, slugging ink on the cloth and upsetting the table setting. Then, he tried to take a grip.

"Odd, isn't it, and enlightening, these peculiar personal reversals?"

Modest's heart sank. He knew some insult was coming. He looked around the table: Lorraine Boe; her ex-husband Brad Gable, now a security guard at BCU; Larry Dawdler, the ever-present consiglieri; and the newcomer. Modest wondered who would be in the firing line.

"Modern pharmacies have everything. But whereas my dear wife, Anna, spends small fortunes on products to remove unwanted hair from her face and arms, our esteemed new friend, Brad Gable, spends even more trying to get hair to grow on his head. If only they could exchange furs."

Anna tried to control her tears. Brad Gable forced a set smile. Modest felt mortified on his mother's behalf and a sneaking sympathy for Brad Gable, expected to act the toady and accept cruel personal insults. Larry Dawdler came to the rescue by returning to the energy assessment. While Groznyy and Dawdler droned on, Modest considered how, when a couple lived through an unhappy marriage, so, too, did their children, their friends and neighbors.

The door-slamming incident between Oliver Swindle and the recalcitrant professor reverberated round the three colleges. Mordred Stickleman was first to exploit it to whip up his colleagues' increasing resentment of Groznyy.

"He listens to no one. Our distinguished scientists working in the labs receive grants based on the existing system of energy assessment. There's bound to be so much for rental space, so much for heat and light. Then come the temps from Scientific Sticklers—childish invaders—to impose new analyses that contradict the existing science contracts with the foundations.

"Wouldn't it have been better, dollar by dollar, to throw the $800,000 of the entire enterprise in one-dollar notes from the highest window of the Great Library of Milhous College to go wherever the wind scattered them?"

Whenever Stickleman spoke against Groznyy to BCU professors, he was speaking to the converted. But Stickleman also sensed he was gaining ground as his words were repeated across campus.

LOVE BITES

One day Hermione found Modest withdrawn until lunch, immersed in his sketchbook. Apologizing for his black mood, he let her see what he had been doing.

When Modest showed Hermione his cartoons, as an incomplete artist herself, she recognized someone with exceptional talent in another field. True, the influences were crystal clear—the pop art school unofficially led by Andy Warhol, Jasper Johns, but especially, here, Roy Lichtenstein with his precise point-clear distillation of strip cartoon adventures.

"It was you, Modest, wasn't it? That satire of the provost's breakfast club that went out in the student paper. How did you get away with it?"

"I didn't. Somehow, I lost the drawing. Then it was all over campus. Papa never knew. I said nothing—even to mama."

"You could make a living with these."

Hermione chose another of Modest's cartoons, a double panel with two drawings—a diptych.

In the left panel the BCU professors were represented not only as the naughty priests and nuns of Carl Orff's *Carmina Burana* or Geoffrey Chaucer's *Canterbury Tales* but also as sophisticated Americans leading lives of oblivious self-indulgence under medieval wimples and turbans. Here was the bumbling Hubble Grove of biology, the billowing Cleverly Forlorn of English, and the outrageously bewigged Paddy Brillo of chemistry. They were framed on either side by the two dyed-haired robotic professors of Earth Sciences who never spoke to one another but instead passed messages on via their secretary.

In this first panel on the left the professors were eating,

drinking, and making merry, oblivious to a dark oval speck in the sky.

But in the second panel, on the right, they were looking upwards and askance at an ominous flying saucer honing in on them from the sky and bearing the legend GROZNYY REFORMS. A little green man, peeping out of the saucer, was shouting, "Okay, you dead beats! I'm coming!"

The overall headline caption was HIT BY A FLYING CHAUCER.

From a student music group, Hermione knew the student publisher of the weekly BCU magazine *Student Babble On*. She took the cartoon to him. Not only would he publish it, but he also wanted more.

"It's perfect. The style is perfect. And another thing: all their names are perfect. It's like their parents named them to grow up as cartoon characters. Fiction couldn't improve on these names. The way they tell you the professors' characteristics helps readers interpret the pictures."

The publisher also invented a press name for Modest the cartoonist: "Something simple, nothing obscure, nothing Russian—Dare Devil."

Since Modest was moving into troubled political waters, he and Hermione agreed it was best that he did his cartoons at her home where she would store them safely away from the prying gaze of his father.

When the diptych was published, it caused another sensation.

Mordred Stickleman did not like being included among the professors as a lanky lachrymose malcontent. However, he knew that his being included might deflect any idea in the Groznyy Gang that he was responsible for bringing the cartoons to light.

Already titillated, students and professors alike eagerly awaited another Dare Devil diptych to drop like a calf from its mother.

As they continued their little private conspiracy, Hermione continued to express delight in Modest's cartoons.

"I just wouldn't know how to start," she said after work one day.

"Yes, you would. Every press cartoonist has the same problem when there's a new kid on the block because his characteristics aren't so well known. But quickly, we get the picture. So cartoonists start with, say, a blank oval for a face. Then, as the new president starts to show his hand, so they respond."

Hermione obligingly drew an oval.

"Take your shape. If it was going to be Franklin Roosevelt what would help?"

"Wheelchair? No, too confining. I know. Jaunty cigarette holder."

Hermione gave this a try but was not impressed.

"Anything else?"

Her eyes lit up.

"Pince-nez eye glasses."

"Try broad shoulders as well."

She did.

"Whadaya think?"

"Well, you've only just started. And you can cheat."

Next day after work, in the Great Library of Milhous College Modest found a famous nineteenth-century cartoon by Thomas Nast, caricaturing President Andrew Johnson. He placed some tracing paper over it for Hermione to trace the outline and add a few details.

"Try this. Cartoons are like other art form. They follow rules. Once you've absorbed the rules, you can fly. In some ways cartoons are easier than conventional drawings. They require not more but less. They invite readers to fill in the blanks by supplying ideas from their own reactions."

Modest took Hermione to a newspaper room that also held magazines, some recent, some older. Leafing through one, he came across a photo of Ronald Reagan on the staircase of Air Force One. He was waving his hat and showing his head shaved on one side after surgery. His wife, Nancy, was looking on horrified at this burst of spontaneity.

"Trace this. Copy it, concentrating on the outlines and some crucial features—Nancy looking aghast, Reagan looking mischievous."

Hermione had not had such fun since kindergarten.

She now thought Modest's face looked more appealing than ever. The lines that appeared when his father was mentioned were now smoothed out. His eyes had started to gleam, basking in the growing tendrils of love.

They knew without asking that they were both virgins. But they felt so close that they wanted to be lovers and make love that night.

Hermione lived in an apartment converted from the loft of a rickety Dutch Colonial style house on the leafy breast of a hill off White Water Avenue. She had gone there to keep an eye on her failing aunt who lived on the first two floors: "It's like Aunt March and Plumfield in *Little Women*."

"Does that mean," asked Modest cheekily, "that you see me as one of Jo's Boys or Little Men?"

"You're making me blush. Anyway, shortly after I came my aunt's health got worse and she went into residential care. I'm the house caretaker until the family decide what to do with it."

Modest and Hermione felt so intimate that they did not mind being inexperienced—that they would fumble with their bodies as well as their clothes. Tender kisses led quickly to heavy caresses and aroused such intense passion that they were swept away. They did not even unlock their embrace after each climax.

Modest's ecstasy as a new lover spilled over into renewed self-belief about his art for as long as he would be able to see to draw.

At the time, Hermione thought she was acting on impulse. Modest always made her smile with joy. Once he mimicked her drawing her panties back up after they had made love. This made her giggle. Modest joined in and they fell on the bed helpless with laughter. Then they undressed and made love again.

Hermione realized that, with this spontaneous laughter and deep affection, she was responding to her deepest feelings. She was so content that, after Modest left that morning, she played the first movement of the Moonlight Sonata straight through without a mistake.

At lunch that day, Modest said, "You've given me back my confidence. I'll apply for more art courses at Cooper Union next year. If they accept you, the courses are free. Then we can be in New York together when you're at Tisch."

After two weeks, Hermione gave Modest her father's ring, a simple gold band. He promised never to take it off.

One fine evening, Mukhtar and Saleem went to a private meeting in the leafy suburban home of Saleem's "uncle," Ace Ferrari, dean of psychology. They went in through the back door into the little kitchen as the chosen few Middle Easterners were discussing the controversies swirling around Provost Groznyy and how this might impact on their long-term, extra-curricular project.

"We are safe," said Ace Ferrari. "This little apology for Ivan the Terrible is an emblem of what is wrong with the western world—especially its political leaders. These professors—they're meant to be intellectuals. But the professors and the untitled princes of the federal government who own them body and soul through research grants, are our antagonists. They are obsessed with their status. If this is the way they think, well, the future truly is ours. We wait."

This was not what Mukhtar wanted to hear.

"The brothers have had enough talk to last this lifetime

and the next," he said. "What are you going to tell us—that Imperial Rome will fall not through us but consumed by its own vices? No, it's time for action."

"Not yet. While the professors of the Opposition Party are devoured by their own envy and the Groznyy Gang is diverted from academic reform by its love of wealth, neither side can see the real danger to their precious western civilization. They can't even take precautions—far less do anything meaningful about it."

After the meeting broke up, the two brothers-in-arms, the dean of psychology and the chair of chemistry, reviewed it. Don Fatale had a different take from the dean on what had been said.

"I think you should give them something to do, divert them from arguing."

Ferrari gave in. He decided to give his little battalion, his greyhounds straining at the leash, something to do. He would aid the case against the provost of BCU by giving him a nasty shock—exploding a minor bomb outside his home. He asked Saleem and two more of his best soldiers to meet him the following night. He got Don Fatale to entice them with an operatic image.

"On a campaign in the town of Kazan, the real Ivan the Terrible got his men to dig some tunnels right under the Kazanka River," the chairman began. "Inside the tunnels, Ivan had his men set off explosive devices with fuses inside candle wax. The men lit the candles. The wax ran to a barrel. The barrel started whirling. It rolled down the tunnel and went off—bang."

"Now, we—you—will get under Milhous Avenue and do something similar but more modest," continued the dean. "Nothing as dramatic as Ivan against the Tartars—just a little bomb. Give Groznyy a scare. Let him think the Opposition Party means business—that they're ready to kill him."

The dean was thinking, "It's a practice run." Aloud, he

said, "I've chosen you because you can control yourselves. The enemies of Islam know just how we can give ourselves away by seeming nervous. You can do better."

When Modest arrived back home early Sunday morning after another night of frantic bliss with Hermione, daylight was returning. Faint streaks of light made the empty roads look pristine before traffic started again. Modest was surprised to see a young man with a truck fixing the drain outside the provost's house.

"Must be an emergency, since it's Sunday," he said to himself.

As Modest went upstairs—quietly he thought because the boards creaked—he heard an explosion outside and smelt acrid fumes. Modest tore down the stairs and ran to the kurb. There was no one else about—just the same young man now on his back in agony outside. He was bleeding. Then he passed out. A woman came out of a Milhous museum across the street.

"Call for an ambulance. This man's been injured in the explosion."

"How did it happen?"

"Dunno. I was coming back from my girlfriend's."

The woman went back into the museum to make the call. Modest could not be sure but he thought he saw splinters in the young man's face, especially around his right eye. Staring more closely, taking in the bulbous nose and the pockmarked skin, he realized it was Saleem, the man from the chemistry lab.

The woman custodian reappeared with a blanket and a pillow. Before she could minister to the wounded chemist, two other Arab men appeared, apparently from nowhere. They wanted to take charge.

"We're Saleem's roommates. We can manage now. Thank you."

"That can't be," said the janitor. "Look at him. His eye's badly hurt. He's streaming blood. We have to get him to hospital."

The arrival of the ambulance interrupted the little dispute.

The first paramedic said, "He's badly injured. He's got to have medical treatment. You're at college, aren't you? You've got insurance. Leave it to the professionals."

The police had also arrived.

"How did this happen?" said the first officer.

The first Arab was quick to answer almost as if he had learnt his words beforehand.

"He dropped his keys in the drain when he was going to the van. He was looking for them with a torch. It must have gone off in his face."

"But you weren't there. You arrived after the accident," said the woman.

"What went off?" said the first officer.

Modest realized that the injured man's friends did not want him treated in hospital. They did not want the police asking questions. As the ambulance trundled away, the friends, looking black as thunder, got into their own car and followed behind.

Modest, who had appreciated his new friend's help in the lab earlier that month, phoned the hospital next day to ask after Saleem, the wounded man. He was surprised to hear that, within an hour, before the medics could inspect him, his friends had bundled Saleem off to a private hospital three towns over.

There, Modest would have been even more surprised to hear the injured man and his friends change their story.

"I was moving a butane gas canister. It exploded in my face," Saleem said.

The overworked doctors at the second hospital bandaged Saleem's wounds and let him discharge himself. In his bolthole apartment, Saleem did not like the phone call from the double-dealing dean.

"This was exactly what we don't want—detonating a bomb too early. Your first test and you fail. What would have happened if this had been New York, eh? You'd have detonated the bomb too early, killing yourself and missing the target. We can't use you. Disappear off the radar."

"Give me one last chance."

"I don't think so. Mukhtar can stay but not you."

"You need us. We can still be of use. You said yourself, 'Every successful detonation is a publicity victory in the war of the worlds.'"

"This wasn't a success. It was an unwanted commercial. Guess I'll have to find myself more nephews."

The dean called the chair of chemistry.

"Saleem's playing a dangerous game. It's one that can only end badly with him getting his fingers burned."

"Like his face?"

"Exactly."

Modest could not rest. With his mind turning over the street incident again and again and his imagination brimming over with images, he thought his next cartoon creation had to be his masterpiece.

In the center were Saleem and Mukhtar, the details of their features reduced to a minimum, but with olive skin, hooked noses like avenging blades, and the unforgiving eyes of psychotic zealots. Amidst a battalion of gloomy chemical bottles and jars, they stood at a crude washbasin stirring up a fizzing mixture to make a primitive bomb. In one side panel two seated policemen with their legs up on a desk were reading the sports pages of a newspaper. In the other panel Groznyy and Dawdler were whiling away their time playing Scrabble.

Above, an airplane had burst in two and was falling to earth.

"I think everyone will get the point," said Hermione. "Short of showing the emperor Nero playing the violin while Rome burns, readers will see apathy from police and politicians while terrorists concoct their deadly explosion. Apathy reigns supreme."

A grave thought struck her.

"Cartoons don't always have to be laugh-out-loud funny," said Hermione. "And I know humor is the most durable form of political comment as well as the most penetrating. But it's difficult—no, impossible—to raise a laugh over the mass murder of innocent men, women, and children. I think we should keep this in reserve—use it later when the atmosphere is right."

After the weekend, Modest and Hermione returned to find the Swindle survey in the process of moving from Science Park to the hospital complex. There they were to work under a new taskmaster.

Whatever the weather, whatever her mood, Hermione always enjoyed her morning bus ride down White Water Avenue through Babel City to Norse Hoven. To her, the winding road was lovely—the way it bent through the suburban-scape of quaint nineteenth-century houses in white or gray shingle. Then there were pastel-colored ranch houses and apartment buildings with cream stucco and red doors.

The mighty reservoir appeared to the west with its elegant swans and cute cygnets before disappearing underground. Later it re-appeared to the east, reflecting the majestic splendor of craggy Great Rock studded with soaring conifer trees. Best of all was the overall impression of traditional, small town America. The continuous stretch of charming buildings on White Water Avenue never got rundown as it entered downtown. There were no tawdry strips, no intrusion of the slums of Louvre Ville to the west.

For Hermione, journeying along White Water Avenue was a comfort.

And she would need comfort that day.

Whatever problems the pseudo-scientific team had with the dry old stick in Science Park was nothing compared with their experience with his alter ego in the hospital complex. This was the aforementioned Ms. Dolly Drum Dong, the woman Mukhtar had mentioned as on his little list of people who would not be missed. Dry Stick Swindle introduced Ms. Dong to the group as "A charmer, a real charmer with a first-class mind and a Chinese husband, also a charmer."

Dolly Drum Dong wore a dark gray women's business suit with the faintest hint of pinstripe, diminutive diamond studs in her ears, and a gold wedding band. She was dressed for what was then the contemporary role of Manhattan office worker—not as a leading player. Dong knew that what would make her look like a best supporting actress in the Big Apple would, in small town America, make her look like a star. Her dress had one meaning for her bosses: subservience; and another for her temps: control. She intended her costume to convey a stark message to her team: "You report to me. I have exacting standards. Measure up or I will bury you."

The giant hospital complex included a base for animal experiments with caged, scrawny primates. On this subject Dong waxed lyrical with vicious ease. Ever the mistress of SM moodiness, this was the perfect subject for her bristling power trip.

"To make our study as complete as possible, we must enter the corridors where they keep the monkeys used in prescription drug experiments. Here we restrict our measurement of length, height, and width from the outer walls to the cages. These little critters look cute and enticing as they clamber to the cage bars toward you. But, as they beseech you for food, keep your distance. These are vicious little critters with sharp teeth and strong arms and hands. They can tear your clothes and bite you so badly your wounds will turn septic."

Every two days the little band of pseudo-scrutinizers had to report individually to Dolly Drum Dong. She would peruse their surveys and the Byzantine mathematical calculations of energy use.

She rebuked Modest in no uncertain terms:

"No, nope, no, that's not it at all; you've multiplied energy use and heat loss together, instead of subtracting the second from the first and then multiplying according to our special mathematical formulas."

She was equally cutting to Hermione. And she said much the same to the other temps one by one as if they were the only individuals at fault. After members of the group began to rationalize Dong's behavior, they opened up to one another with comparable stories. But Mukhtar, who seemed to have the goods on her, was no longer there.

Some temps buckled under the strain of her carping and asked their agencies to be transferred. Some she asked their agencies to fire. Within ten days the original band of forty temps had shrunk to a dozen.

What tipped Modest and Hermione from suppressed fury with Dolly Drum Dong into aggressive ridicule was her treatment of a single mom with three kids that was so nasty that it amounted to constructive dismissal.

Of course, Modest had an outstanding string to his bow. Supported by Hermione's loyalty and drive, he was ready to let his artistic arrow fly straight to its target. He revised his next cartoon several times before Hermione took it to the student newspaper.

Under the caption SWINDLE AND SCIENCE stood Dolly Drum Dong, legs astride in dominatrix pose. She was in her Manhattan gray cloud suit but her armbands and a peaked cap boasted Nazi swastikas. Above her upper lip she sported a tiny Hitler mustache.

To her left Oliver Swindle struggled with a cascade of numbers on a primitive abacus and a puny slate, crying out in exasperation, "I'd rather die than call Dr. G. for help."

Between them plodded a weary band of temps marching to an outsize French machine of decapitation labeled "Mam'zelle Guillotine." To the right, professors in Science Park responded with irritation and contempt.

Although publication of the cartoon provoked more ridicule of Groznyy, the response from Scientific Sticklers and Groznyy was silence.

But Modest was doubly unfortunate in his enemies. The next sections he was supposed to scrutinize by himself for the survey were in the hospital's eye infirmary. Modest dreaded going to Dr. Chicago's clinic. He did not want anyone there to recall he had been there for laser surgery.

No one remembered him. But he did upset Dr. Chicago's secretary. Even Modest could tell that this Lee Aison was devoted to her face and figure. In her scheme of beauty, that waif-like figure had to be anorexic. This she had achieved by stringent dieting and treadmill exercise.

Don Fatale, the chair of chemistry, had not forgotten what might have been costly carelessness by Saleem over the airplane plan and the computer message. Neither had he forgotten that it was Modest Groznyy who had exposed this security lapse even if Saleem had swept the lab clean before the police arrived. It was also young Groznyy who had found Saleem wounded outside his home after the bomb plan miscarried. Besides, Modest had once caricatured his friend the dean and his pompadour hair in a newspaper cartoon. Both dean and chair wanted Modest out of the way.

Chance gave them the opportunity.

Dr. Chicago had sent Don Fatale a few sample bottles of a new contact lens solution. Some patients had had an adverse reaction to the solution. Would the chair of chemistry help the eye clinic by analyzing the contents to see if there was a problem? Of course! Don Fatale gave the sample bottles to Mukhtar.

"You know, these could be very useful little bottles," said Mukhtar as he fondled one. "Very adaptable. Any passenger could take a tiny bottle with contact lens solution on board a plane—whatever is in them."

Fatale decided to hand his report—that the solution was safe—personally to Dr. Chicago. It was part of the dean and the chair's charm offensive: disarm the enemy with a calculated display of niceness.

Dr. Chicago was not in. But that did not matter. Someone else was.

When he handed the report to Dr. Chicago's secretary there he was: the moppet-haired son of the hateful Groznyy. And he was taking notes. She was engrossed in what was a private conversation with one of her girl friends. Modest could also not help but overhear Lee's endless phone calls.

"Carmine, I know classical music doesn't turn you on but you would have had a laugh at this. When his date pulled out, Dr. Chicago asked me to go to this concert at Milhous College. The music was by students. When they finished the third piece, the conductor said they would have to repeat it because, first time round, the choir had sung it in the wrong key. Imagine!"

In a flash, Fatale saw how he could manipulate one situation to solve the other: get rid of Modest Groznyy and his hair. Fatale moved. It was all so easy: engage the wan secretary in idle chitchat.

"Another pawn," the chairman thought. "No wonder her lunch mates refer to this Lee and her noontime salad as the stick and carrot."

All he had to say was, "We'd better be careful what we

say. The young guy over there from the science survey—he's taking down everything. I'll say no more. Shush."

Then he was gone. But the chair had left Lee Aison in a panic. She had her own agenda in Dr. Chicago's clinic. Were her minor lapses, her private phone calls, being noted for use against her? She had better get in first as soon as the young whippersnapper had left.

Modest was concentrating on complex measurements but he sensed Lee Aison's resentment. He was beginning to dislike himself for being part of the shabby enterprise.

That would not be his problem for long.

At home before dinner that night, Modest took a phone call from Dolly Drum Dong at her sickly sweetest.

"Here we go," thought Modest, expecting to be rebuked for the cartoon. But no.

"Modest, there has been a complaint of rudeness made against you by a member of hospital staff. She said that you made dismissive remarks."

"Who said this?"

"I cannot say because you are contracted indirectly to us by the Human Resources office. But I cannot have members of our team discrediting us by rudeness."

"What is supposed to have happened?"

"Professor Fatale says you referred to this poor secretary and her lunch as the stick and carrot. I was once a student of your esteemed father. I'm sure he will be very disappointed in you."

Modest was nonplussed. When he called Hermione, she put her finger on the problem.

"It's that Lee Aison woman. When you were in her office, you saw or heard her doing or saying something that she shouldn't have. She's tried to discredit you by saying you were rude. Then this Dong woman sees you as a threat. She's changing the focus to rudeness since she can't fault your work without getting rid of everyone else."

No sooner had Modest put down the phone than it rang. It was Lorraine Boe. The BCU manager of Human Resources first said she had called about some error in his pay check. Then, all of a sudden, Lorraine said, "I'm sorry, Modest but we have to let you go. We have no choice when the client says so."

As Modest was pondering this, Lorraine asked, "Is this Dong woman on a power trip or what? What is her problem?"

He said, "What happened to me was blisteringly unfair. The whole scheme is a farrago. Let's just say that, in this dog-and-fox scam, if Oliver Swindle isn't crafty enough to be a fox, Dolly Drum Dong is over-qualified for the role of bitch."

"I think it's a cat and a fox in *Pinocchio* but I get your point," said Lo.

THE NEW HOLLY WOOD

Modest now had the problem of how to earn his keep if he started art studies at Cooper Union in the fall. At least he was going to stay near Hermione.

When they met he said to her, "I've had an idea that would solve two problems—your being in the city for Tisch School and earning your living nearby. My father had a crazy aunt, Babulenka. Years ago, she founded this niche restaurant in Manhattan. She bequeathed the restaurant to her major domo. That's Benny Vincenzo. My father thought he'd get his hands on it. He was livid when he failed. But he still uses it for business deals. Benny is looking for a youngster to help him run the place. That could be you."

"But I've no experience of catering."

"With Benny, that'll be an asset. He wants someone fresh whom he can train in his way. Besides, if you're thinking of a career in arts administration that means you've got transferable skills."

Among the reasons Hermione liked Modest so much was that he put other people's interests before his own.

"So, if we go into the city on Friday—cheer you up with a jazz night in Greenwich Village like we've sometimes said—we could call at the restaurant first?"

"Right. I'll prepare the ground with Benny. It'll be an informal interview."

As they crossed the Norse Hoven Green, they noticed a middle-aged, hung-over drunk slumped over on a bench with his head in his hands. He was wearing the sort of preppy clothes he must have worn when he was young. He looked wasted. They turned away.

Ashley Bedfellow Burns's descent into his own toxic hell of perpetual drunkenness had made him the most unwanted guest of his old friends, the one who always over-stayed his reluctant welcome and needled his harried hosts beyond exasperation.

"Pity me! Pity me," he sometimes said aloud.

But there was no answer. Everywhere he went he was always in solitary confinement. But his mind always had the same accusations, always the same bitter reproaches. Before her funeral, they had asked him to look on his mother one last time. But he had not had the courage. Instead, he kept imagining her face wreathed in white hairs strewn across her cheeks, moistened with water like a drowned girl in a pre-Raphaelite painting. Her face came to him again and again in a vivid dream. It was as if her expressionless face was accusing him.

He had done nothing with his life, nothing with his career. And, in all but name, he had killed his mother, his true supporter, and his best friend. He had killed her as surely as if he, himself, had exposed her to Death by Cold. He did not want to believe in God. But now his academic cap was like a crown of thorns. It was as if above him hovered an invisible shroud of his own doom or he was an animal kept in a pit. He reached for the bottle.

"Poor soul," thought Hermione as she glanced back at the un-remembered drunk.

Modest was as good as his word to Hermione about the niche restaurant. But Hermione was not impressed with the rundown exterior of the Golden Cockerel. Despite facing south, on an early evening still sunny, the building looked somber, uncared for.

"So, you're Modest's little friend whom he's recommend-ing to help me out," was how Benny greeted Hermione.

He motioned to Modest to sit in the reception area while he gave Hermione a guided tour.

The dark ground floor had a narrow, twisting hall with a

minute but well-stocked bar where Modest helped himself and Hermione to whiskey sours, while Hermione followed the burly Benny.

"There's a printed menu left at the front door—Modest will show you—along with souvenir white marbles with the restaurant's logo: a golden cockerel," Benny added, handing her two such marbles.

"However," Benny continued with smiling insistence, "I advise guests what to select."

Hermione sat in a corner and watched as Benny took orders, oiling his way from table to table with his unassuming introduction: "We have some nice items today."

As she surveyed the scene, Hermione grasped that the meals were all streamlined efficiency at minimum cost for maximum profit: a special lentil soup; a green salad; the cheapest vegetables, such as zucchini, to decorate the supposed *haut cuisine* of meat and fish dishes.

"Chicken is safe for everyone but there's no pork since that might offend Jewish and Muslim guests," added Benny.

"The steak is always marinated so skillfully that your knife goes through it as if it's butter," said Modest as he downed a second whiskey sour, as if it, too, were butter.

From her seat, Hermione could not help overhearing two diplomat guests speaking. The older one said to the younger, "Beats me how Benny Vincenzo got his sticky fingers on this joint. Legend has it that he comes from a family of New Jersey landlords; that he moved from liberal arts at an exclusive local university to the hurly-burly world of catering, becoming an indispensable factotum to Princess Glinskaya. She willed him the business on her death. But it's difficult to credit."

His companion answered *sotto voce* but Hermione heard it clear enough.

"A more sinister version has it that the princess was ready to pass her business to someone in her family—he's at a university in New England. What I heard was that Benny, protected by Cosa Nostra, was able to force the Glinskaya lawyer into altering the princess's will with a murky transfer of deeds. They do say"—and here he lowered his voice—"that a crucial signatory had his writing hand broken so his signature could never be the same again."

"But who knows the truth?"

Benny recognised the voice as belonging to the Know-All from the UN.

Hermione shivered. What was she getting into? When she took stock again, it seemed that the dinner clients and restaurant staff formed a court around Benny Vincenzo. Benny beckoned to her and then to Modest in the bar.

"You may want to hide now. Your father will be here soon with some special guests. From the musicians' gallery you can observe how we do things. But you have to stay silent. Modest, you know the way."

From their secluded vantage point in the musicians' gallery upstairs Modest and Hermione got a different perspective of the early evening scene with its patterns of client and staff movement across the faded red carpet. Everything was choreographed.

"When you dine here, without you noticing it, you never wait for service for the service is seamless," remarked Modest.

It was true. Once diners finished a course, their plates disappeared. Nor did waiters hover unwanted or heeding a guest's every word.

"Nor is there confusion if two parties arrive together. Benny manages to chart their progress along the corridor to the dining room—perhaps by polite conversation— or care over coats, or a seemingly chance remark over a scarf."

Indeed, from downstairs they heard Benny say in the corridor about someone's scarf, "Such iridescent colors!"

"That's one of his favorites. Benny says that sort of thing so that meals can be staged according to his own timetable."

This had come from Benny's observation that it was neither the public nor the food that came first. What was paramount was the process that had to be orderly and timed in sequence for preparing, cooking, and serving the courses. And it was this efficiency that pleased everyone.

Modest was thinking how much better Benny ran the restaurant than his father ran BCU. Then his father arrived with his entourage. Larry Dawdler guided two women to the table. One was the ample Lorraine Boe. The other was a chic Manhattan professional.

"I remember some conversation between Lorraine and papa about appointing a hotshot public relations dame whom he wants to give BCU a sharper profile. I bet that's her."

Hermione admired the immaculately turned out Manhattan pro: "Hitchcock blonde," she whispered.

While Benny was taking their orders, Modest and Hermione realized that they both knew what the other was thinking: the college provost and the city restaurateur were eyeing one another warily.

Cesare Groznyy and Benny Vincenzo were both hyper-sensitive individuals who felt themselves on the periphery of social life in New York. They both had an uneasy relationship with Manhattan. In their minds they inhabited its twilight world whose fantastic side they used to get what they wanted. Cesare Groznyy wanted to amass a fortune and be hailed as an academic leader. Benny Vincenzo wanted easy access to the pleasures of the flesh. Cesare and Benny both shared a natural gift for comedy and impersonation, an ability to capture a character in a couple of swift gestures. But Groznyy lacked Benny's warmth and depth of understanding.

Modest identified more characters below.

"At the table across the room, there's father's other fixer, Brad Gable, there—the little fat man in the charcoal suit. He's Lorraine Boe's ex-husband. His guest will be one of the singers or Broadway gypsies he plays away with. He brings these singers along to the Golden Cockerel as if he's their promoter. Usually, what happens is that they see the other clients as too old, or too uncool. When they see that the chances of paparazzi photographers being present are negligible, they make an excuse and leave."

Just then, Brad Gable's guest turned round to take stock. Now Modest had an unpleasant shock.

"It's her. It's that Lee Aison who had me fired. I'm sure of it."

Hermione sensed that Modest was having an unpleasant jolt to his stomach. She whispered, "Bottle blonde and cheap perfume."

His response surprised her.

"I don't think so," said Modest. "That albino blonde color is natural. I bet her folks are from Ukraine. Look at the cut of her features."

Hermione fell silent. Modest had not said anything like that about Lee Aison when he told her of his contretemps in the eye clinic. She sensed something had shifted inside Modest.

There they were assembled in the restaurant with the banal dramatic irony of some TV soap opera: university provost and toadies at one table; aspirant artists hidden on the musicians' balcony above; wannabe star and shady protector at another table; and mein host, the master puppeteer, gliding around the floor with a dose of smarm.

Almost as if she was obeying Modest's scenario of the ungrateful protégée to the letter, downstairs Lee Aison rose abruptly, calling for her wrap. Brad Gable shrugged to the two men opposite.

As she whisked herself out of the main dining area, Lee

sensed that umpteen pairs of eyes were appraising her. Unaware of the commotion she had caused upstairs, all she could see were two middle-aged men opposite looking at her rather than their own guests.

"How corny," she thought. "Two more geezers."

Lee knew the score. Then, for no apparent reason, just before she made her exit, she told the tubby manager that she would return momentarily to the dining room to glance at the central chandelier—so iridescent—and check just in case she might have left her scarf—so diaphanous.

As Lee stood briefly at the entrance to the main dining room, she gave the scene the benefit of a final glance. The man with the dissolute face glanced back. He winked at her—lasciviously, she chuckled to herself. She knew he was mouthing pleasantries in Russian. Not so pleasant, she thought, if the other lady guests knew what was being said. There were *double entendre* comparisons between a cello and the lovely body of a young woman. In a trice, Lee was gone but not forgotten.

Modest and Hermione realized it was time for them to leave for the jazz club if they were going to get a good seat. Hermione could tell Modest was unsettled by the brief appearance of his adversary. She did not know if she had been hired at the Golden Cockerel until Benny said, "Come next week, starting on Tuesday and we'll have a trial period for a month."

With that, Hermione, like Modest, was free from Scientific Sticklers.

Modest and Hermione then took the Lexington Avenue subway to Grand Central, crossed the city via the Times Square Shuttle and then caught the Number 1 local train down to Greenwich Village. Steered by Modest's experience, they managed the hop-skip-and-jump walk along West 12th Street to where it crossed 8th Avenue. Thus they arrived at the jazz club in forty minutes flat. Hermione was impressed with Modest's mastery of Manhattan. But she was apprehensive that another shock was in store.

They scrambled down the rickety circular stairs into a smoky cellar jazz bar. Its burnt-sienna décor was punctuated here and there by odd Café-de-Paris touches with wooden candelabras and wall lights with pink shades decorated by red tassels. By contrast, the tables and chairs were rudimentary while the bar was all glistening chrome, silvery steel, and a slab of imitation black marble. Hermione was not surprised that the prices were not rudimentary. How could she make her ten-dollar whiskey last the night?

"I must really love him to sit through this music at these prices."

To Hermione's weary eyes the bar's smoky atmosphere was like the proverbial pea soup of a London fog. But Modest was clearly excited since he was a real jazz aficionado. That was, perhaps, enough to divert him from his own problems. She continued her thought: Modest was among many people who yearned for tender companionship amidst the lonely canyons of a modern city. But these people were still lonely—despite the seductive but compassionless blare of their preferred siren, jazz.

Modest was reading her thoughts.

"These are things we do for our friends—go to movies and shows we're not interested in and—"

"Jazz clubs," added Hermione.

They sat through several sets featuring improvized solos by different instrumentalists. In between drumming his fingers on the table, Modest tried to enlighten Hermione on the finer points of their skill. Since her agenda was to break his depression and woo him as best she could, an hour passed while she nursed her cocktail before their second upset of the evening.

When the singer arrived in her little black dress, they did

not see her at first, partly because they were sitting to one side and partly because of the smoky atmosphere. But when the singer opened her mouth, they were stopped in their tracks. It was Lee Aison.

When she finished "Stormy Weather" the spontaneous applause came so hard on her last phrases that it was clear here was an audience that could not hold itself back any longer. Then she sang a 1960s hit, "Sealed with a Kiss." Smiling as she finished a lovely turn of phrase, it seemed Lee was giving her song to an intoxicated Greenwich Village.

Modest was gazing enraptured. Hermione listened with growing disbelief. Surely, this was Dr. Chicago's Lee Aison, the blonde they had espied in the restaurant who had had Modest fired from the survey? But, surely, this could not be right? This stage artist had talent and magnetism.

"I've got to give it to her. Stunning stage presence," said Hermione.

"Shush," said a voice from behind.

Hermione turned round and saw a bespectacled man with receding curly hair. He met her glance coldly and took off his eyeglasses to polish them as a sign for her to stay in her place.

But he waxed lyrical to his companion.

"She has tender, sweet tones as well as blue notes. She sings like a lark and has darker tones in reserve to color phrases."

"Critic," mouthed Modest to Hermione.

Hermione whispered back, "I think it's the guy who disrupted the little lecture on Palestine."

"Shush," repeated the voice, this time more insistently.

As she came offstage, Lee noticed an Arab-looking man standing at the crowded bar and swinging a Bloody Mary in time to the band's exit music. He had a huge nose and dark, liquid, come-hither eyes. Despite a clumsy bandage on one cheek, he still had the swaggering style of unreality Dr.

Chicago told her he associated with oil sheiks. Modest would have recognized him as Saleem.

Brad noticed Lee and the Arab exchange glances. He said to show who was in control, "He's far from a model Muslim, what with these rumors of roughing up his wife and trying to pull married women."

Lee shrugged.

Just before she had to step onstage for her final set, she heard the club manager say to Brad, "If she goes on singing like this, in five years she won't have any voice left."

Lee felt her confidence drain away. She was even more jolted by the reply of her gum-chewing promoter: "In five years, I'll find someone else."

In an instant, Lee was onstage. With her performance, she had to draw in perhaps eighty people. She had to hide her hot anger without harming her performance or it would be over in a single night, not five years.

How Lee got through the set, she never knew, although she had heard the phrase "auto pilot" used about jaded actors in long-running Broadway shows who were surprised to hear themselves deliver their next line when they thought they had dried. Like Broadway gypsies, Lee did finish the set. Doubts raced through her mind. Was she singing recklessly and losing her voice? Had she been too naive about managers and promoters all along? But Lee was no naïf, she told herself. She was a cultured artist who excelled at carefully rehearsed, under-rehearsed charm.

She could not hear what her newest fan was saying about her.

"She's special," Modest told Hermione. "What about her range in her three sets this evening? Her elegiac singing catches the heartbeat of blues numbers and the heartache inside them. She's got sure show-biz sense. She knows how to balance dreamy numbers with upbeat breezy ones."

"Who's the critic now?" thought Hermione, who said

lamely, "She dances a fine line between glamor and parody, I'll give her that."

They heard the man behind them say to his partner, "The human voice is a frail instrument. How precious and rare is an artist like her who can use it with dexterity and insight. This Lee Aison has everything."

That was not what Lee herself realized. Goaded by the manager's crude dismissal and her promoter's double-dealing response, Lee came offstage challenged about her future.

On an impulse she almost leaped back on stage and whispered something to the leader of the little combo. Then she embarked on an unprepared encore: "I'm Gonna Wash That Man Right Outa My Hair," from *South Pacific*. When she got to the brief spoken aside, "Get the picture," she darted a mean look at Brad Gable who juddered at the hinted subtext. He shuddered as Lee mimed washing her hair because he had so little and because her subtle defiance suggested that here was a more formidable artist than he had bargained for.

Having brought the house down, Lee got ready to leave. As clients complimented her, it was as if she were expected to encourage everyone there with an assured gracious manner, by a flutter of her false eyelashes, so that they would tell their friends. Lee found herself pretending laughter at one stale joke and held-back tears at the next pathetic tale.

When she moved to the exit, the man with the bedroom eyes and the bulbous nose was suddenly at her side. Even though she was leaving on Brad Gable's arm, he asked her if she would go on a date with him.

"Pretty lady," he cooed. "Wouldn't you like to go out with me—see the town? We can make even more beautiful music together."

"What chutzpa," Lee thought as she sailed out, smiling to

no one in particular. Then she checked herself. This Arab man, whoever he was, was playing a part, but then so was Brad Gable, as she had just found out, and, for that matter, so was she.

Still at their little table, Hermione realized that her swain now hankered after Lee Aison, his enemy of earlier that week, but she kept quiet. She put on an assumed smile of contentment. She sensed that Modest was fighting his sudden attraction. But her new sense of competition, roused by Modest's unexpected new love, had started to make the two of them look at one another critically.

Hermione knew Modest was a true jazz aficionado. She had already gathered that Modest's father was overbearing and kept him on a tight rein so that his enthusiasm for jazz and blues was his emotional outlet. Nevertheless, she started to be annoyed by Modest's wide knowledge of jazz performances, his ability to compare so many different interpretations of "Summertime." As a jazz critic, Modest left Hermione at the starting post and it hurt.

Modest began to find Hermione's pose of girlish absent-mindedness and her negligible knowledge of jazz a bore. He thought her shallow for thinking Lee Aison was a blonde bimbo when he could sense she was a rarity, a natural blonde Ukrainian artist with the assured stage persona of a jazz pro.

Modest and Hermione traveled home to New England on Metro North in silence punctuated only by Hermione's forlorn determination to keep matters upbeat. She made agreeable comments on what they could see from the train window: a sudden logjam of traffic from a road to the west and, later, a surplus of cars at a service station just off the interstate.

Back in Norse Hoven they shared the taxi from the station in a glum mood. When Modest dropped Hermione off at her home, there was no goodbye kiss, not even a peck. All he said was, "Good luck for Tuesday."

This dismissal was out of character for Modest.

Hermione knew that, while they both had the love bug, she for him, he for this Lee, they would remain distant.

On Monday morning, Lee Aison was surprised to receive a dozen red roses at Dr. Chicago's eye clinic. When she phoned the number on the card, she realized this Modest was more than a star-struck kid. She was impressed to learn his father really was provost of Babel City University. She was embarrassed that she had caused him grief in his temp job and was won over by their similar Russian backgrounds.

"You're right. No one else ever guessed it. My dad was from Kiev. But once he settled here with an American wife he did not want his kids hankering after the old country. No Russian spoken at home, no family history retold. We were born stateside and were to be one hundred percent Yankee."

At work Lee was often too preoccupied with her toilette to notice the variety of people who passed through Dr. Chicago's clinic—patients, colleagues, and other staff. But that morning when she overheard Dr. Chicago complaining about something to another doctor, she heard the tart retort from his colleague: "That's show business for you: management first, public second, artists last."

This set Lee thinking about Brad's jibe, her place in society, her failed relationships, and what singing in a series of smoke-filled cabarets must be doing to her voice.

As she half listened to the hubbub in the clinic, she recognized that the lives of Dr. Chicago and his colleagues were just as unsatisfactory as hers—he who could never commit to a relationship with any of his girlfriends and who always threw in his cards when he did not have a perfect hand. Then during her lunch break Lee heard on the office radio a midday chat show about star singers who had either changed or adapted their names: how Doris Kapelhoff had become Doris Day, how Caryn Johnson had become Whoopi

Goldberg, and how Lillian Klott had become sweet Georgia Brown, the first Nancy in *Oliver!*

She wondered if Doris Day's career would have opened up if she had accepted the role of sex predator Mrs. Robinson in the film of *The Graduate*. Would the moviemakers have let Doris Day sing the "Mrs. Robinson" song in the film? Would she have escaped sexcapade comedies before they went out of fashion?

What prodded Lee's curiosity more was a comment that the higher film stars rose and the greater the pressure on them to carry movies, the more convenient it became for them to distinguish between their old and new personas; how they tried to think of their public names and screen personas as public property; and how they wanted to think that, within them, there still existed their original private selves into which they could retreat off camera.

One of the radio pundits related all this to the Greek myth of the Cypriot sculptor Pygmalion who had made a lovely statue and then fallen in love with it. The goddess Aphrodite took pity on him and brought Galatea to life. This interpretation prompted Lee to use her lunch hour next day to go to the public library on the Norse Hoven Green. She looked up "Pygmalion" in the *Encyclopaedia Britannica*.

Lee read how Pygmalion was devoted to his world of silent statues in preference to the rash girls around him. The goddess punished them by releasing their sexuality to such excess that they took on and satisfied all comers. Degraded and exhausted, they shriveled up and Aphrodite turned them into barren rocks.

Lee did not need any interpretation from Dr. Chicago to realize that, if she continued as she was doing, what was left of her youth would be spent; her voice would be in tatters, and her body as barren as the rocks of Amathus. Worse, she would have done all this in service to men who would find someone else in five years' time.

Lee noticed gaps in the shelves of the library encyclopedias. Then her eye caught an untidy pile of volumes on a table opposite. Surely that was Ace Ferrari, dean of psychology at BCU, whom she recognized from his occasional visits to Dr. Chicago? She remembered his olive complexion, flashing eyes, and gleaming teeth, all adorned by a jet-black pompadour hairstyle. Had he swiveled his chair away from the table so that he would not have to acknowledge her? How odd it was that he should use the town library on the Norse Hoven Green, when he must have many more books to choose from in the bullring library on the BCU campus.

Opposite her, immersed though he was, the dean of psychology had noticed Dr. Chicago's secretary. He hoped she had not remembered him. Ace Ferrari wanted to read uninterrupted and not be seen.

His choice of subject, one as full of reinvention as hers, was Ivan the Terrible. He had started to read about the Russian despot ever since academic troublemaker Mordred Stickleman had suggested that not only Ivan's name but also his career were Cesare Groznyy's model and inspiration. Away from campus, so that no one could chance upon what he was after, Ferrari was looking for clues as to what might be Groznyy's next move. If he and his allies were to use the Opposition Party's feud with Groznyy to further their own interests, he had better study the career of the original Ivan the Terrible.

What he read alarmed him.

He skimmed through the entries on Ivan IV's personal life, his serial marriages. Were there seven or eight?

"That's the way Christian husbands behave," he said to himself.

To his later, bitter regret, he also dismissed that part of the entry about Ivan killing his own son as something like a horror movie—even with the evidence of Soviet dictator

Joseph Stalin's barbarous treatment of his sons mentioned in a cross reference.

In the notes on political infighting in Ivan's court, Ferrari saw parallels between the court of Ivan Groznyy and the backbiting of the Groznyy Gang at BCU.

What the dean took from all this was that Cesare Groznyy was bent on self-destruction and that, inwardly, he wanted to fail. So, the furor over Groznyy's imperial style was a perfect smokescreen for his own and his allies' double dealing.

What drew Dean Ferrari up sharp were the accounts of Ivan the Terrible's wars on his eastern front. It was not the details that alerted him: it was Ivan's all-encompassing grasp of global politics. First, there was a threat from the east. Second, Ivan resolved to tackle it. Third, Ivan was able to use it to set his permanent stamp on Russian history. Could Groznyy flush him and his Oryx Party out?

Lee Aison had a bad hand, a damned poor hand at cards, but she had to play with the cards she had. She had to take control of her life. And she would start by reinventing her stage persona, by changing her name.

At home, she went back to her few reference books on movies. First were stars who had changed their names. With steely determination, Lee Aison methodically ransacked the variants of the stars who became superwomen. She worked out what had turned them into icons. She knew that much of Audrey Hepburn's success had been as a clotheshorse for Givenchy and how her sleek black dress, chignon, and cigarette holder had defined her screen persona in *Breakfast at Tiffany's*. This was a character with another past and another made-up name: Holly Golightly.

Then there were the Hollywood stars who could not sing the songs of their roles in musicals—Deborah Kerr, Natalie Wood, and Audrey Hepburn, again—at least not all the way through. Marni Nixon had sung for them.

It still rankled: "In five years I'll find someone else."

So that was it—what Lee wanted—a time limit. Not "How long is a piece of string?" but "five years" and no extension for good behavior.

When Lee went back to the entry on Natalie Wood, it hit her. Not that Natalie Wood had started life as Natalie Wood but as Natalie Zacharenko whom a Hollywood studio had renamed. It came to her like a thunderclap. Holly and Wood. She would become Holly Wood. And a Holly Wood outside motion pictures, a singer with a name you could never forget.

The name was ideal. It was evocative yet it was ordinary. And it contained the seeds of its own self-promotion. When she ran it by Carmine, her girl friend was even more enthusiastic than she was.

"Honey, it's just right. Every time a TV commercial, a journalist, or someone in casual conversation mentions 'Hollywood,' they'll be promoting you. Your name will be on everyone's lips. It's perfect. And you're perfectly equipped."

She was, too. Next morning Lee-Holly looked at herself in the mirror with the sun boring its way through the blanched shade. Its soft light enhanced her pale face as she applied her makeup. Then she brushed her hair. Her tresses rippled over her head, veiling its shape with their sheen. Her new name gave Holly Wood extra confidence, extra pizzazz, and extra artistic depth when she sang the next weekend at Badger's Sett in downtown Norse Hoven.

So, into the drama of the modern Ivan the Terrible and his opponents, inside and outside the academic world, stepped a new talent, a symbol of the eternal feminine upon whom men projected their fantasies, her name not only the name of a place but also a landscape of mind.

When they had something important to discuss, the dean of psychology and the chair of chemistry were as likely to do so in an open place as in one of their homes, where comings and goings might be noticed. Thus they took in the view from Great Rock, surveying the panorama of the twin cities below.

"I told Saleem I'd find myself more nephews," said Ace Ferrari.

"Is that wise?" was Don Fatale's response. "We can try and fast track young guys from Pakistan here on student visas. But if we do it too often, the INS will start to take notice. I think we'd do better turning young guys who are here already. There is someone at BCU in the treasurer's office: Darko Delizio."

"Darko Delizio? What sort of name is that?"

"'Darko' is a shortened form of the Serbo-Croat word for Theodore—meaning loved by God. 'Delizio' is an Italian word and name that means exactly what you think it does. Anyway, Darko is from Yugoslavia. His grandparents were Muslim refugees from Albania during World War II. Yugoslavia under Tito welcomed them. Now there's all sorts of trouble brewing in the Balkans and southeast Europe. Darko Delizio is Christian now. But I think he will revert to Islam. He's on good terms with Mukhtar. Divided family, divided loyalties—I think we can turn him. Another thing— he speaks several languages."

Before he attended Lee-Holly's next gig, Modest read a letter in a local alternative paper praising this new jazz singer while criticizing the nightclub audience of two weeks ago for stinting their appreciation.

"With the soon-to-be renamed Holly Wood," claimed the correspondent, "the weekend audience in Manhattan had heard genius in their midst but it had gone unacknowledged and unappreciated." He compared Lee-Holly's care over words in her singing of jazz and blues standards and her uncanny ability to sing precisely on the note to the skill of the most meticulous classical singers. He singled out the way Lee-Holly had handled the falling melodic line of "Send in the Clowns" as an "astounding intermingling of musical effortlessness and dramatic tension."

Modest scanned the letter to get to the signature: "Augustus Revisor." The name meant nothing to him but he wondered if, just possibly, it belonged to the man who had shushed him up, and who had overturned chairs at the lecture on the Palestinians.

Modest was even more won over during the new Holly Wood's appearance at Badger's Sett. As she moved through her well-paced selection, alternating fast and slow numbers, she proved herself soulful in wistful songs, flirtatious in scat singing, and nonchalant in upbeat numbers. While she was singing "I Got Rhythm," she might have been thrown off balance by the surprising sound of a baby smuggled into the club who had started crying. Instead of freezing, the new Holly Wood took it as a challenge. In her improvized section of scat singing, she introduced mock sounds of a baby whimpering and chortling while finding time to chide the parent by adding, "Couldn't you have left the little fellow at home?" in time to the music, thereby doubling her applause at the end.

Modest was agog with excitement.

Before her second set, and again for no reason she could think of, Holly noticed yet another swarthy man with flashing teeth, a bulging nose, and restless black eyes lounging by the bar.

Modest also noticed Mukhtar and with him another much better-looking man whom he did not know, maybe Arabic, maybe Latin.

"Hi, Mukhtar, I sure didn't expect to see you here. I didn't know you liked jazz. How's Saleem doing? Better, I hope."

Mukhtar did not answer directly.

"I'm just blending in."

"Not assimilating—just blending in," Modest thought.

Between sets, the young blades, Mukhtar and his friend, tried to woo the re-christened Holly Wood. They sent her a scrawled note via the bartender: "Don't be shy—beautiful voice with charming eyes. Give us a signal. When you sing, send two flashes in our direction."

Modest noticed the interaction. He guessed what was happening and—since there was no reply—what was not happening. That was good: the new Holly Wood was not rising to the bait. While the band played on, Modest pondered a discrepancy between belief and behavior. The Arab contingent, as he now called them, made occasional references to religion, about how Islam, like other great religions, taught the values of faithfulness and compassion, about the dignity of humankind, and respect due to others. But in these guys' role—or was it a disguise?—as students, they acted like other emancipated—or was it dissipated?—western students. They were at college for sex and drugs and rock 'n' roll. They might have wives far away but they lived for the present like opportunists with girlfriends. If, and when, they had enough money, they made an exhibition of themselves, enjoying some goodies of western consumer society.

In Modest's distinctive eyesight, they were shadowy figures all right. He became convinced they were playing roles in American society. Their outward form was commitment to the American dream: belief in bourgeois values of hearth and home, capitalism as a natural meritocracy, and, therefore, loyalty to a corporate career path. But, if they also seemed the opposite—that they were tearaways—their pose was simple: they were going through a phase, like so many carefree, young American males.

With his inner eyesight still that of a quick-fire artist, Modest got the impression that, whether wild and abandoned socially or reliable and sober professionally, what drove these young men was some inner desperation. Yes, there was something desperate about their gaiety. If they were living as if there were no tomorrow it was because they knew there was no tomorrow. While it looked as if they seized their pleasures wherever desire took them, what really drove them was a compulsion fueled by self-loathing.

That evening in Badger's Sett it was like the same audience surprise in the Greenwich Village jazz club two weeks beforehand—the same joy of recognition among jazz aficionados for a major vocal talent. Modest knew it would always be the same for him. Every time he saw Holly Wood, he wanted his hands to roam over her perfect shape and undo the ribbon-like tresses in her hair. He found he could not sleep for thinking of her. He sighed when he thought of her tender lips. Many people were good-looking but, with her, it was as if she had a light under her skin. Her presence irradiated her surroundings as she captivated everyone with her very glance.

The two Arab steeds were still hovering at the edge of the little stage. Mukhtar said, "Give us a moment. We're fans. Just show your affection. We know how to make you happy."

Holly decided to have some fun at the expense of her competing swains. For her encore, she returned to *South Pacific*. This time her number, "I'm in Love with a Wonderful Guy," might, superficially, seem to confirm her returning the Arabs' affection, or, at least, interest in one of the men who adored her. But which one? There were several. Modest was in more anguish than ever. The other suitors were way more experienced. What would Modest do? What could he do?

After her gig, as Holly left, again on Brad Gable's arm, Mukhtar's better-looking friend who was now standing with him near the exit, said, "You don't have to take us seriously."

Mukhtar added, teasingly, "We're two lovable mad men. Look us over. Have a heart, my friend is just back from the wars."

Holly did not need Brad Gable's usual warning not to say anything. Mukhtar's friend struck her. Good-looking maybe, yet he had the wily face of a fox but the pleading eyes of a haunted spaniel.

Mukhtar and his friend plucked imaginary glasses of liquor from the bar, swigged down the contents, grimaced as if they had drunk poison and were in agony. This made Holly laugh as she left. She wondered where the good-looking man had stolen his lines and his stage movements. Mukhtar said to his friend, "C'mon, Darko, there are plenty more fish in the sea. You've got *Cosi fan tutte* on the brain."

Unseen at the back of the smoky bar, Dr. Chicago sat enthralled. For the first time he realized that the new Holly, his secretary Lee, had an amazing voice. Her range was like an elevator, soaring to the skies and then plumbing the depths. And she was like a skilled trapeze acrobat when it came to her technique in scales, scoops, and scat singing. Everything Holly sang was full of meaning and nuance— ecstasy and joy, anguish and anger. And whatever she sang, her voice was instantly recognizable.

As Modest was leaving, he noticed Mukhtar had his arm round some redhead, while his buddy, Darko, was seated on a bar stool, staring into middle distance. Darko Delizio was an experienced lover, used to wooing and discarding women as he chose. Now he had this irritating love bug for Holly that made him forget his family.

Mukhtar said to Darko, "What's up? Forget the college accounts. Give your mind a break from work. Lighten up. It's time to party." Then he said to the girl, "C'mon, baby, it's rom-com, chick-flick time."

Next day, Mukhtar took a risk. Without any introduction,

he asked Darko, "Wouldn't you like to hear more about our great mission?"

Darko nodded.

Hermione started work at the Golden Cockerel with some trepidation. But the process of learning from Benny and helping take stock at the restaurant slowly eased her out of the emotional shock of Modest leaving her.

One morning, when she was in the upstairs private room, she heard scuffled sounds from above, although she knew Benny was not in his third floor apartment. She thought of the threatening houses in paintings by Edward Hopper and houses with dark secrets by novelist Charlotte Brontë. When she asked Benny about the unexplained noises off, he answered matter-of-factly, "It must be rats—they get into the wall cavities."

Hermione thought it odd that a restaurateur should be so dismissive of a health risk but said no more.

"I'll explain," Benny told the princess, "when we've come to trust her."

Hermione found herself being gradually coaxed out of any love-sick depression by the sights and sounds of Midtown Manhattan. It was not simply that anyone needed to keep their wits about them as they moved among the jostling traffic and pedestrians on streets and avenues. It was something more. She appreciated that the beauty of New York was in its strength and vitality and not in perfect cityscape panoramas of skyscrapers.

She remembered Modest telling her something about artist Edward Hopper's ambiguous attitude to the raw disorder of New York. Modest had told her how Hopper had honed impressionist-like painting techniques to highlight themes of loneliness and alienation in what were, on the surface, realistic paintings. For the present, Hermione felt different. Sometimes, when she was running errands, she would turn a corner and find herself looking anew at the Chrysler Building or another skyscraper. Suddenly, there they were, peeping out from, or above, other buildings and peering down at her from an unsuspected angle. It was as if they were showing off their distinctive style and also their humanizing aspects. Like other yuppies, it seemed to Hermione that New York was whispering in her ear, "This is now your town. You belong here."

MODEST PROPOSAL

Modest was in moderate torment. He knew he would not pine away for love of Holly. He knew there was no point in sighing. Yet he was so lovelorn that he wanted to give her some tokens beyond red roses so that she would always have some reminder of his devotion. He sent her a jazz CD of a new local trio and some CD reissues of original cast recordings of Broadway musicals.

Holly decided to let Modest date her in earnest. He was to be part of her strategy of reinvention. After all, it would soon be spring. Holly could tell this Modest would be good for her career—give her status. His charming manners made him more than presentable. As to sex, he would have to put a lot of money into the slot machine before he hit that jackpot. Even more, marriage was for the birds. Easy does it until her future was secure.

This Modest Groznyy could wine and dine her, make her look better when she went to a gig by being so agreeable in preference to the balding graybeards like Brad Gable she usually had to put up with. Being with someone in his early twenties, ten years younger than she was, would take five years off her age, and make her whole package—voice, artistry, and style—more marketable.

But it was Modest's sincerity that won people over to him. Her girl friend, Carmine, told Holly that she had heard around campus what his mother believed: "Once Modest makes friends, they are friends for life." And when they went to gigs, Holly realized it was true: Modest inspired spontaneous affection. He told her that, years ago, one of the Groznyys' housekeepers had called him "Modest-and-a-half" because "he was too much trouble for one little boy." She had meant it—and his mother had taken it—as a fond family joke. As she started to fall for him, Holly understood why: Modest was better than she had bargained for.

So far, so good for Holly Wood. The first big hurdle would be the horror of Meet the Folks but she counted on her stage experience to win over his mother.

Brad also knew the score. He counted on Holly coming back to him for promotion.

Modest knew he had to move fast or risk losing Holly and he was lost for words. However, he was his father's son. He found the words he needed. When he rifled through librettos in his mother's opera LP sets, he bypassed the A, B, and C of opera—*Aida*, *Boheme*, and *Carmen*—in favor of those beginning with M—not for Modest—but for *Manon*. From his study door, his father noted what he was doing.

Before one of her gigs, Holly caught Modest speaking silently to himself as he waited patiently—modestly in fact—for her while she said good night on the phone to her folks in another state.

He answered her unspoken question.

"I was trying to, working it out, rehearsing really, how to tell my father about us and how to put things."

Holly was taken aback.

"We've only known one another a few weeks."

155

"Yes but I know my mind—and his. Words that come from the bottom of my heart will not move him."

"You're apprehensive?"

She was surprised this sophisticated word popped out of her mouth.

"His temper is legendary."

Modest decided if they got sidetracked about his father, he would never get to the point. Holly understood that she must never say a word against Modest's father and mother, even if she was provoked. Modest returned to his imaginary presentation drawn from the libretto of *Manon*:

"Her real name is Lee Aison and her stage name is Holly Wood. No one has a voice more pleasing than hers. When she sings, her voice draws a whole audience in so everyone catches their breath. She sings like an exotic bird. Oh, yes, she is lovely and graceful. She is everything I love. And, yes, she is a little older than me."

Modest paused in case this was tactless. Holly Wood said nothing.

"She still has youth and beauty. Her heart is open to life in all its fullness. There is no one whose manner is so charming, so tender."

"Is all this true? Do you really love me like that?"

"Love you? I adore you."

"You don't have to do this. Isn't it enough that we are falling for one another?"

"No, not enough, you must be my wife."

"Your wife? Not 'We must get married.' Must be your wife. You really want that?"

"With all my heart."

"Come and kiss me."

When they tore apart from one another's arms, Holly said gently to Modest, "If you really feel like that about us, you must tell Hermione. It's only fair."

Modest frowned but he knew what Holly said was just.

He tugged at the ring Hermione had given him. Holly had just assumed it was some family or fraternity ring. Modest did not tell her anything different. He did not know how he would go about telling Hermione it was over. So he did what he had done with his little rehearsed speech to his father—but which he had still not delivered. He consulted his mother's romantic operas—back to M, this time for *Mastersingers*.

Hermione was beginning to think she would never hear from Modest again. When he did call her, he began with stilted chit-chat. Her response was equally reserved. Then it came out like a torrent.

"Listen, Hermione, I know you're upset. I'm sorry. I can't help what has happened. You were becoming my dearest friend. How can I ever thank you for helping me regain my confidence about my eyesight? What would my life be like without my having met you? I should choose you. But I've fallen in love. The way I feel about Holly, I had no choice."

Hermione thought he must have written down the words first and that he was simply reading them out aloud. But she still felt the pull of his voice. The sound of it drew her to him even though she resented the borrowed novelette style.

"Well, all the Agony Aunts in the world are going to tell me what pain I'll suffer if we continue with you feeling the way you do for this Holly."

"She is the most beautiful woman, inside and out."

But Modest could not bring himself to return Hermione's ring to her. She did not want him to.

Modest and his proposal would end with the death of this novice lover. He was a lamb to slaughter, indeed, as outsmarted fiancé, as victim of delayed infanticide, and as a symbol of the way society can devour idealistic youth and its hopes.

*

First, Modest faced his next challenge.

"There's something I have to tell you about myself."

Holly braced herself.

"I have poor eyesight—I'm very short-sighted. There are some extra problems. I can't even remember how much laser surgery I've had—and at Dr. Chicago's clinic."

Holly felt ashamed. She had been so preoccupied with her career. Here was this boy who simply wanted to adore her. She melted. For a brief moment, she wanted it to be the two of them against the world. She knew the feelings he had aroused might not last. But the draw Modest exerted ran deep. At this instant, she wanted him far more than any sensible choice.

Despite all her previous hesitation, Holly began to teach Modest physically what she had learned from her previous lovers. She encouraged him and their physical love was intense.

Day by day, week after week, somehow their love affair ignited the link between her voice and her artistry, her skill and her interpretations, so that her performances gained depth and intensity. The two became inseparable just as Modest and Holly themselves became inseparable. She always thought of him when she sang. And she was ready to stare down what she knew would be his father's hostility and contempt.

Yet Holly was relieved that she managed not to yield to the temptation to tell Modest her innermost secret. It was a dark secret lodged inside like shrapnel in a wound. It could burst open at any time.

It was the damned table leg that did it—provoked two fatal crimes.

Earlier, when Anna and Groznyy were redecorating the Bedfellow Burns house Anna had suppressed her own desire to soften the black-and-white, steel-and-chrome interior design Groznyy insisted upon. But, as domestic wear-and-tear gradually but insistently wore at the edges of the furnishings and chipped away the pristine perfection of his ultra-sterile choices, she started to compensate for his glacial design with softening touches of her own: easy cushions in pastel colors, shiny mauve vases with cut flowers, imitation eighteenth-century ceramic shepherds. She planned to turn the house from an unending cascade of harsh lines into something more like a country cottage.

Among Anna's chosen *objets d'art* was a fake onyx coffee table. It had a burnt-sienna marble seam effect rippling across its apple-green plastic slab top. Its frame was gilded and its legs were bowed. Inspecting it closely in the Manhattan store in Union Square, Anna had detected a flaw—some broken ornamentation below the rim. To her surprise, she finagled an appreciable price reduction.

Once it was delivered, Anna tried her best to site the table to optimum effect below a bedroom window. She placed a Hong Kong plaster shell basket decorated with flowers and crabs in vermilion, olive green, and rose white, atop her new side table.

From the start, Groznyy hated the tacky bourgeois ornamental table and he particularly hated that the onyx was plastic.

Humiliated, Anna decided to retire the offensive table to Bee Flute's outer office in the provost's suite. There it was again—the damned table. Groznyy was so livid that in a particularly childish outburst he kicked the table so hard that one of the legs came off. Bee tidied the table in a side alcove just inside the provost's office to await repair.

It was a week before Memorial Day, traditionally the day of Commencement at BCU, when students took their degrees and distinguished people received honorary degrees. President Franklin Miller had been summoned to Washington on unspecified business. Thus Provost Cesare

Groznyy was to preside in his place. In that week, when BCU was bustling about with Commencement arrangements, Modest introduced his girlfriend to his parents. They were to have dinner before a concert.

Holly knew she had to make a good impression on Modest's mother. Since this was the beginning of summer, she chose a floral print. She adorned her summer dress with delicate braids of ribbon highlighting her pert breasts and emphasizing her slender waist. Even so, and despite her maturing artistic skills, she felt queasy.

When Modest guided Holly round the presidential corridor, she thought she heard a sigh before they knocked on the door of the provost's office. It was, to her, a musical sigh, like a blues lament underlined by a woodwind solo. Through the half-open door of an inner chamber, there seemed to be someone protesting about losing their job, about how working there was like torture. Holly imagined the hidden scene in a dark red color.

At Holly's introduction to Modest's parents, all three members of the Groznyy family stared hard at her: Modest with unqualified love, his parents with loathing so extreme that Modest put it down to jealousy on his father's side and a sad realization from his mother that she had to let him go—let him choose his partner for life. They were staring one to another in different modes of outrage, disbelief, and confusion.

What Anna was thinking was, "No. Not now. Not this." She felt weak, then a twinge in her back, then dizzy, and then she knew. "It's come back again. Dr. Squires said it might: pneumonia."

There was a tap on the door. Bee Flute bumbled in.

"Modest, dear, there's a call for you from Lorraine Boe—something about rectifying a mistake in your last pay check from the survey. You can take the call on Darko Delizio's phone in the treasurer's office down the corridor."

Even when he was livid, Groznyy's flickering mind could catch others' stray thoughts. He noticed a flicker of recognition from Holly when Bee mentioned sub treasurer Darko.

"I'll be back momentarily," said Modest as he slipped out. Bee was back in the room.

"Mrs. Groznyy, Dr. Squires is on the line. Would you like to take the call in private in my office?"

Anna was filled with profound embarrassment. The interruption was a relief. She was out of the inner office in a trice, leaving father and daughter-in-law elect alone. Groznyy turned to Holly. He bared his teeth.

"I don't know what you think you're doing, Miss Lee Aison, Miss Holly Wood, Miss Gold Digger, or whatever else you call yourself these days—Miss Adventure. But this situation, Miss Understanding, ends right here and now. You, a secretary by day, a jazz singer by night! Does that mean a genius by day and a beauty by night or is it the other way round? You can never be a trophy wife to our adored son, the mother of any grandchild of mine. No, Miss Match. The social barriers between blue blood, blue chip, and blue-collar and poor white trash like you are insurmountable. Insurmountable, do you hear? So, this modest proposal will not end with you making a meal out of a babe in the woods."

He was glaring at her with a look of contempt meant to freeze.

"You have a nerve coming here, d'ya know that? You, a paltry never-has-been dressed in your shower curtain, trying to stare us out: big Miss Take! Pretend to Modest you're in love? At best you're a bitch in heat. Do you hear me loud and clear?"

Holly felt blood rising in her cheeks. She knew she had to take a grip on herself until Modest and Anna returned. She had been playing a dangerous game. She had known that all along. She tried to assume a pose of being nonchalant. She sat down on the arm of the leather sofa to the side of the onyx-topped table. This pretend nonchalance provoked Groznyy even more.

"Stand up, you damn bitch. Stand while I'm speaking to you and you listen."

"I'm listening and I'm comfortable as I am."

"I'll give you comfortable."

Groznyy bent down and grabbed the spare table leg and moved close to her. Holly did not flinch even though she expected him to hit her. She knew she had to stare him down whatever the cost. He clutched the fuller, upper part of the broken leg in his right hand and pointed the lower part, the tiny pointed claw foot, at her cheek. He controlled himself, touched her face, and grazed her skin. Holly still did not flinch. Instead, she shifted slightly on the sofa ledge and crossed her legs. This tiny gesture of defiance pushed him over the edge. Groznyy grabbed her face just below where he had grazed the skin and held it tight. That was enough to unbalance her. She tumbled off the sofa. He thrust her down farther on to the thick-pile apple-green carpet. She gasped for air. For a few moments, she was unconscious.

Groznyy stood over her and said quietly, "Now, don't you dare Miss Behave, don't Miss Construe this little Miss Hap."

Bee came in, quickly took in the scene of collapsed guest, broken table leg, and Groznyy's stance, and surmised what must have happened.

Modest came back from Darko Delizio's desk in the treasurer's office where he had learned that he was going to get some significant back pay. He found his mother in tears on a chair. Holly was on the floor—her head propped up with a cushion and being comforted by Bee. His father was sorting out papers on his desk.

Bee said, "Modest, dear. There's been an accident. Holly

162

tripped on the carpet. She's in pain. I've called for an ambulance."

His father murmured a word beginning with "Miss" but the others only half heard him.

When the paramedics arrived and took Holly off to the hospital, Bee thought she had better get the offending onyx table and its detached leg back to the Groznyy house where it could not tell tales.

Brad Gable drove Modest to the Milhous Hospital. They sat side by side in stony silence. Dr. Chicago met them in reception. He was not his usual unflappable self.

"Modest, they told me what happened. I came as soon as I could. I'm sorry. Holly has lost the baby. They've given her a mild sedative. She's sleeping. She will feel better tomorrow and be back to normal in a few days."

Modest could barely take it all in: accident, fall, baby, and miscarriage.

While Holly was still asleep, Modest called his mother. Their conversation was staccato, interrupted by his father's offstage remarks:

"What the hell did she think she was doing? Hasn't he heard the expression 'poor white trash'? She's forty if she's a day.

"Holly Wood? Holly Wood? That's not the name of a singer, a chant-tootsie: it's an address. Whatever next? She might as well call herself Beverly Hills, or Glenn Close, or Veronica Lake. Her name is no better than making Pearl Harbor a woman rather than the site of a national disaster. Whatever next? Hope Springs? Alice Springs, maybe? Sara Sota? Even Rose Garden?"

Next Modest heard Larry Dawdler in the background add more vaudeville asides: "Stella Artois? Polly Styrene? Coral Reef?"

"Better Penny Lane—no—Penny Dreadful," sneered Groznyy.

Groznyy then grabbed the phone from Anna and yelled at Modest, "Well, my dear son, this supposedly innocent flirtation of tender lovers will not be rewarded with marriage, oh no."

Modest put down the handset.

Later, in the hospital, sitting in the chair beside his sleeping girlfriend, he whispered, "I'm so sorry. I will love you forever. I promise this will make us stronger together."

And that was what it did.

Back in her apartment a few days later when she was more comfortable and more collected, it was Holly who roused herself to soothe Modest as he struggled to overcome his whimpering over his impossible, deadly father.

"He's a brute and I let him do this to you, to us."

"Modest, don't blame yourself. And don't blame him overmuch no matter how loathsome we think him right now. This might have happened anyways, without him and his anger. For us to get through this, we have to do what he would do—at least on the surface—play it cool."

Then Holly saw that Modest Groznyy was, indeed, his father's son. His face visibly tightened, as if he was summing up his boy's courage not to face down his father but to face a future beyond and without him even if it meant leaving his mother behind. He never cried again. They simply held hands over the kitchen table. It really was the two of them united against the world and whatever it might throw at them.

"I will always stay with you—for as long as you want me. Next week, we must do what you would do onstage: play our parts. We have to show the world we are united, together, inseparable. That means we go out together, that we are seen together. And we begin by going to the BCU Commencement as a couple. I never cared for Commencement before."

"Me neither," said Holly, "But, then, I never went to college. But, of course, you knew that and it didn't bother you."

"But now Commencement suits our purpose. It's a showing all right. In the meantime, I will say nothing to my father in hell. Here actions must speak louder than any words I could find."

It was a Commencement tradition at BCU that the provost's wife carried a special bouquet of red roses. She would give a rose from the bouquet to each guest receiving an honorary degree. When Modest arrived at his family home early on Memorial Day at the same time as the florist's delivery man, he took the bouquet and bounded up the stairs to hand it to his mother. He had missed Anna and seized this chance to give her this as a token of reconciliation.

Cesare and Anna Stasinova Groznyy were in their bedroom putting finishing touches to their formal attire. When Modest went through the open bedroom door, he could tell that his father was fit to be tied. At first he thought this was because Anna had returned the onyx table and its telltale leg to the window alcove. Then Modest saw copies of what he guessed was the BCU student paper scattered around. Groznyy practically tore the bouquet out of Modest's hands and threw it on the floor. Anna retrieved it.

"So, it was you all the time—the so-dexterous and insightful cartoonist who has been lampooning me, the trustees, the professors, and everyone else at BCU who makes the university work just as well as it does, oh yes. Don't even try to deny it. So you thought you would add fuel to the fire stoked by my enemies. Your timing could not have been worse when the eyes of the world are on us at Commencement. You thought you would get away with it, did you?"

With that, Groznyy picked up one of the folded papers and struck Modest across the face, then his head and shoulders.

"And how do I know this, Four Eyes? Through your precious Dr. Chicago. When Larry, who *is* faithful, went to the dear doctor for a routine eye examination and sang your praises, Dr. Chicago explained that even people with serious eye problems can excel in the visual arts, oh yes."

Here Groznyy mimicked a mincing medic.

"You have this serious eye condition, apparently, oh yes, but you still manage to be a dazzling cartoonist, oh yes, dazzling beyond belief, apparently. Forget the cartoons of Leonardo and Goya, for at Babel City we have the genius of Modest Groznyy. Genius! Your drawings are the talk of the campus, apparently. Oh yes, of course, it's meant to be a secret but, since Larry is part of my charmed circle and has known you for years, he must know, oh yes. So the guileless, gullible doctor spilled the beans."

"Cesare, please," said Anna, beside herself with concern for her son.

"Don't try and get out of it. I know a serpent when I feel its sting."

At that, Groznyy realized his hand had been scratched by a stray thorn in the bouquet and sucked the wound.

Modest had to suppress a smile.

"Oh yes, your intentions were good. Above suspicion! Expose the worthy Oliver Swindle, one of the few scientists we can rely on to help take us forward. And for what?"

Cesare had one foot off and one foot on. He stubbed his stockinged foot against the offending table. This time Modest could not suppress a tiny chuckle.

"Laughing, dammit, you young cur? You, Modest-and-a-half, bringing your harlot here, just before our crucial ceremony. Don't 'Papa' me."

The vehemence Modest felt got the better of him. In a

flash, he understood that his father had murmured "Miss Carriage" on that fatal day. His face flooded with anger and contempt. Nevertheless, Modest stuck to the script he had already agreed with Holly: no mention of her miscarriage; no mention of whose fault it was—yet.

"The survey is ridiculous. It doesn't need me to show it up. The guys carrying out the survey are not energy experts, papa, they're temps paid seven dollars an hour. If you pay peanuts, you get monkeys."

This cheap jibe hit home. Groznyy bent down. On impulse, he seized the detested broken leg from the hated onyx table. He held it up threateningly as if it were a lighted torch.

Modest was now in full flight.

"There's a devilish presumption in everything you say or do: how brave, how wise, how important, but never, of course, how selfless"—he paused before his next jibe—"or how pointless your life has been—destruction and despair personified.

"You are a hundred times worse than the greatest betrayers of religion—Judas, Caiaphas, and all the rotten popes of history. Not any of them killed their grandchild and rejoiced in it."

"Grandchild, my ass! You think a little push did it? Didn't it occur to you that this poor little, failed never-has-been-and-never-will-be has had a bigger career with abortions from her failed romances—as many as there are shells on the seashore—and that's no exaggeration—than as a singer? So many abortions that she never can go to term with a child!"

"That's a lie."

"She's playing you for a fool, Four Eyes. She gets you fired, then she wraps you round her little finger! Grow up already, you damn simpleton. The only man who sticks by her is the clueless Dr. Chicago. Even his supposedly platonic adoration has to come from favors freely rendered."

His father's insults, rattled off with sure-fire abandon, left Modest exasperated beyond tears into a white-hot fury that he had never known. He stretched himself to deliver, somehow, a lethal verbal blow to stun his damn father into silence.

"Groznyy—man of destiny! Don't make me laugh! Everyone in the whole wide world fated to love you? What a mockery! You, who have never known the flame of passion? Kiss my ass!"

Anna had never seen her husband angrier.

But then he got even more livid.

"What's that on your finger?" he rasped at Modest.

It glittered in a ray of sunshine as if to say, "I dare you."

"A tawdry ring? A love token from the damned chant-tootsie? We'll see about that."

That really was it.

He pulled Modest close to him. While his son quivered, he used his left hand to grasp Modest's hand. With his right hand, he tugged the ring till it was off. Then he threw it across the room, with a bitter reproach, "Like that awful song says, 'Toot-toot-tootsie, goodbye.' Toot-toot-tootsie should have said, 'So long,' so long ago.'"

Brandishing the table leg, Cesare knocked Modest hard in the testicles. As his son stumbled, Cesare struck him twice across the shoulders. As Modest collapsed, Cesare whacked him twice on the left side of his face with such savagery that Modest was more than out cold. So insensate was Groznyy that he went on kicking his son with one shoe on and pummeling him with the other foot halfway out of the bedroom and into the corridor. There was blood everywhere and a killing silence of recognition.

Cesare Groznyy and Anna Stasinova stared at one another. She wanted to say, "We have to get help. I have to stay with Modest—till we get help." But she found she could not speak—not even a croak.

The bouquet was spattered with blood and crushed out of shape. Groznyy stamped on it.

"Leave it. I'll explain to the guests it wasn't up to standard."

Cesare started to tidy himself to leave. He said matter-of-factly, "Like the English Royals, duty first. Do you hear me? No. It will look suspicious if you are not at Commencement."

Anna wanted to summon up her pent-up anger but she was now catatonic. Groznyy grabbed her by the arm so tight she thought she would stop breathing.

The doorbell rang.

Groznyy and Anna were staring at the body and again at one another. There was no pretending they were out. They both knew who it was. It was the chauffeuse ahead of schedule to take them to Commencement.

Groznyy's fuming red-purple face that had only just apparently expanded like a bulbous satire of a pig now, just as suddenly, began to narrow. Almost like a chameleon, it returned to its accustomed pallor. The swelling diminished rapidly as if Groznyy had taken a swift-acting dose of anti-inflammatory drugs for gout. His face was tightening as if it were being drawn together in an ultra-rapid facelift.

The doorbell rang again.

Cesare pulled himself together. He dragged the immobile body of his son back into the bedroom.

Then Groznyy was back at the window. He opened it. Turning to Anna with a look like thunder, he motioned to her to say nothing.

"Lyra, we'll be down directly."

He closed the window. Anna Stasinova was already fully dressed. Groznyy still needed to put on his other dress shoe.

"Not a word. This is Commencement. Our public duty comes first. We'll see to Modest after it's over."

Anna was still dumb. It was with more than fright.

"Pull yourself together. Play your part as Caesar's wife. There's scores of camera crews—the press—outside."

He did not need to say anything more. With his shoes on but the laces still undone, he pulled Anna after him. He remembered to take the key out of the bedroom door and lock it from the outside. Then he pocketed the key. He pushed Anna Stasinova down the stairs.

At the front door, he assumed a glacial smile. Just before he opened it, he said through gritted teeth, "Remember the last tsar and tsarina had a son sick with hemophilia. Often the tsarevitch was bleeding but they went to official functions with perfect decorum. No one outside the family was any the wiser. Play your part. Say nothing."

He opened the door with a flourish and hailed the chauffeuse, Lyra, as if nothing had happened.

As they drove sedately to the La Crosse playing field, the shock of what she had just witnessed deepened Anna's catatonic state. His voice droned on in the car. She could work out her words, "Remember how he fell, first to his knees, and then flat on his face when you hit him with the broken table leg?" But she still could not speak. He could.

"We're not perfect. Neither of us. None of us has clean hands."

How Groznyy sailed through Commencement, Anna could not fathom.

There was the parade of deans and other lackeys, the ceremonial open tent on the La Crosse playing field, the decorated dais for dignitaries and recipients of honorary degrees. There were rows upon rows of green fold-up chairs, each anointed with expectant rosy-faced siblings and plumped-up parents in floral-print frocks or shirts. There were batteries of family cameras, and those of the university camera crews. Above it all, a benign sun smiled down as if it were some primeval fate holding the destiny of Dr. G. in its enigmatic smile.

Cesare Groznyy was good at suppressing his fears in public. The presentation of self in his exultant life had always been paramount to him. It was far more important than compassion, tenderness, or mercy. He did not know if his son was grievously wounded or already dead, but, if he was, this was an inconvenience to be surmounted. Some people noticed blood on his hand and specks on his shoes.

The mangled body crumpled on the bedroom floor in the provost's house was still a human being. Badly wounded, but coming out of the devastating physical and emotional shock of his father's attack, Modest gradually regained painful consciousness.

Sticky with his own blood, he could not see, only feel.

In his dim, boyish, courageous way, he knew he had to get help. He did not want to touch or tender the bloated swellings and what must be gashes on his head and face where his father had struck him with the broken table leg. The pain was acute. The pain lower down where his father had kicked him senseless was sharp and blunt together. The taste in his mouth was bitter as blood and sap from his internal wounds rose inside him and seemed to choke his throat. He wanted to cough and retch but the effort was too painful.

Worse, Modest could not see. At first he thought that night must have fallen. But dimly he heard street noises of daytime movement. Was this what Dr. Chicago had warned him about? Was it blows on the head that had caused the retinas in his eyes to come apart? Or was it that his face had swollen so much that the flesh was covering his eyes?

During the Commencement ceremony with Lyra at her side near the dais on the La Crosse field, it hit Anna even harder than when it happened. She had raised her beloved son, Modest, for her damned husband to beat within an inch of his life, maybe to kill, and then walk away. The emotional wasteland of her marriage now seemed not just lonely but also threatening. It was as though she was living in a desert and would die of exhaustion, thirst, and desperation all at once.

Professors' wives who knew Anna realized she was unwell. They knew she had had recurrent bouts of pneumonia. When one noticed specks of blood on her sleeve, she assumed Anna had been coughing up blood. They thought it valiant of her to attend Commencement at all. They interpreted her palpable fear as stoicism against medical odds. Thus, paralyzed, Anna Stasinova got through the ceremony, gripping hard onto the steel arms of her chair. She wondered how safe Modest would be till they got help, what lies Cesare would concoct to cover his crime. Surely, after the ceremony, she could escape to comfort her son, to hold him in her arms. One thing was for sure. Once they were through this, she would, somehow, find the courage to escape the sham of her loveless marriage, even if she were to be left alone in dire poverty.

As he played his role in the abject matinee ceremony, behind Groznyy's eyes there flickered notions, plans, and any ruse by which he could escape his fate, killer of his own son.

"I will do such things. I will do them and make them work for me."

That was what he thought without being able to attribute the words or appreciate the helplessness that they disclosed.

Fate had different ideas. Chance would both save and condemn him. Chance and opportunity would obliterate her.

ORDEAL

Discarded professor Ashley Bedfellow Burns felt remorseless Saturn hastening his own death. His body still yearned for sensuous pleasures that had always eluded him. Now Ashley felt Death was beckoning to him through an open window.

"Don't be afraid. Life has worn you out. Come to me. You're feeling quieter now. That's a sure sign that your suffering is almost at an end."

He would become a human fireball.

No obituary would be sufficient.

Everyone was out attending Commencement. Ashley laughed to himself as he thought of the ridiculous ceremonial robes of the deans and professors. Their awkward black-and-white costumes turned such supposed sophisticates into a collection of mint humbugs.

His immolation would not only be a worthy self-sacrifice but also retribution against the man who epitomized everything wrong with academia in general and Babel City University in particular.

He had intended to commit suicide in the provost's house, his house stolen from him. Then he thought it might be impossible to get inside. He considered the driveway but he knew he might be stopped before he could do that. Trying to walk steadily while inebriated was difficult.

Wood was stacked outside for a new house extension planned by the damned provost. Ashley sprinkled the woodpile with kerosene. He was glad he had brought two cans.

The dining room was next to the woodpile—piled so high that it blocked the side window. That was good. When Ashley changed his mind and dared to go in, he would not be seen. And the fire would be bigger. Even so, he was surprised to find that the back door was not locked. He went in as silently as he could into the dining room. Good wood there.

"What's holding me back?"

Above, Modest was paralyzed with fear and pain together. He tried to move but the pain thudded all the way through his head and across his shoulders. Still lying on his back, when he moved his right arm cautiously, he struck something hard and spindly. Modest realized he did not even know where he was. Upstairs or down? All he could remember was his father's furious face being right in his own, then retreating as he grasped his throat and face together and twisted them. Then his father's leering face had retreated more as he started to beat and kick him again.

Suddenly, Modest felt a mighty convulsion surging through him. It must be bile. It seemed about to explode in his mouth. Again he tried to rise to vomit. But the extreme pain made him rigid once again. He managed to call "H." Was it for help or for Holly? His last thought was of Hermione.

Oblivion followed a moment later. His blood stifled him.

Modest lay motionless and extinct.

Everything would burn. Downstairs Ashley pulled one of the imitation Queen Anne chairs away from the table. Its eloquent bowlegs were fake but nice. He took a deep breath and opened the second can of fuel. He anointed himself. Then, he groped for the lighter in his pocket. He clicked it. But it did not light. He clicked it again. This time, it lit. Relief. He took the lighter to the soaked table.

The blaze was intense. He thought he could hear shouts. Alarm. Bedlam. That would teach them. Then he lit himself. Woof. Drunk though he was, the pain was severe. The fumes and smoke were overpowering. Hell was burning. Was it always this intense? The blaze seemed to be saying, "I am still your friend and I will deliver you."

He cried out, "Help! Help me! You gotta save me!"

There was a mighty sound like a thunderclap. Ashley was startled by it. He seemed to hear the inner voice of Death:

"Aren't you in rapture? It's just midday heat blowing over you. You silly old fool! Got you! Stupid, wretched little man. Am I warming you up sufficiently? What a colossal fool you were to drink your life away! Midday burns fierce, tearing your agony and grief. All you want is oblivion. Hot as toast or hot as hell?"

His last thought was, "I did not know fuel was so expensive."

Explosion.

Modest had told Holly it would be best if she waited for him in the enclosure at the La Crosse field for Commencement, which they would watch together. They would be seen. After the ceremony, they could start to plan their future. Holly Wood held her place, all the time bothered that the beating sun would melt her makeup and cursing the young whippersnapper for being so late. Her mother had told her never to chase a man, never to show she was anxious when she was dating someone. She waited half an hour and looked at her watch again. Only five minutes had passed.

How could she have been so wrong about him? She had thought Modest was reliable. By now the stands were so full it might be impossible to move. She sat fuming and she knew she was being ostentatious about it. She felt her neighbors pitied her. This heightened her distress of being isolated even though the Commencement field was so crowded. The sun was beating so hard that she felt dizzy. Modest had promised to bring a pack with water. Where in hell was he?

"Something wrong dear?" asked a middle-aged woman to her left. "Has your date let you down? Held up in traffic more like. It's Memorial Day. Folks don't always allow for congestion on the highway."

Holly was alone in her thoughts. The ceremony passed like a blur. No, she was not wrong about Modest. Someone so sweet would not stand her up. Something had gone wrong. It must be something to do with his leering father. But there he was up on the dais with the other phonies.

Someone behind her yelled, "Fire! Fire to the west!"

Holly was just one of hundreds of people all turning in unison to the west. Sure enough, there was belching smoke above the trees.

Just as suddenly as the silent fumes and the distant cries of alarm, came the foggy blare of a loudspeaker, indistinct in actual words but with a message crystal clear to a captive audience:

"This is the fire marshal. There is a fire to the west on Milhous Avenue. There is no immediate danger on this field here. However, as a precaution, we have to clear the area. Stay in your places until the marshals call your row for orderly evacuation to the east."

The message was not complete before a suffused panic set in. For no reason Holly could think of—certainly not fear for her own safety—she felt sick in the pit of her stomach, worse than before her first gig in Manhattan years ago. People were clambering out of their rows, jostling one another with a confused hubbub. Conflicting directives competed for attention:

"Hold fast until your row is called"; "Move in an orderly fashion to the west away from the police cordon"; "Avoid the trees"; and "Await further instructions."

As the hubbub intensified, it swelled to a bedlam of protest and fear. Old legs unaccustomed to speed and young legs unaccustomed to measured pace moved with common purpose but uneven haste. This ragged human crocodile of anxiety dragged the unsettled Holly Wood along with them.

Hermione was alone with her thoughts. In the late afternoon she had gone to the gym, more to have something to do than to exercise. She felt empty, drained, as if she had given herself away by letting down her guard with Modest. She mounted the treadmill without thinking, set a time limit, a gradient, and a speed on the monitor and began to jog. She glanced at one of the TV screens aloft. Another city fire at the beginning of summer, she thought, as she saw billowing smoke above trees.

Surely that was Holy Cross Church?

When someone turned the sound up, she caught the words.

"Today, Memorial Day, the first day of summer, a fire has destroyed some houses around Babel City University. The blaze spread quickly across homes built mainly of wood. Fanned by sudden winds, the inferno leaped out of control, leaving a dozen families homeless and without their belongings. They only had the clothes they were wearing when they escaped the flames. Even Holy Cross Church was badly damaged."

Hermione was surprised, then anxious.

"Has anything happened to Modest?" she wondered. "Is he safe?"

Then she heard: "Among the people missing is Modest Groznyy, twenty-two-year-old son of Provost Cesare Groznyy of Babel City University."

Her house had never seemed so lonely as it did that evening. Hermione needed to concentrate on something. She played the piano part of Richard Strauss's *Burlesque* so hard that her knuckles felt raw.

*

177

After his fit of anger and his determination to evade detection came Groznyy's long hours of abject realization.

The various refugees from the fire came to stay the night in the downtown hotel of a nationwide chain.

Anna, still mute, sat bolt upright on the bed and stared into space, petrified, with vacant piercing eyes.

Groznyy started to prowl around. In the late hours he went up to the top floor that was closed to the public after a visit from pest exterminators. In an empty room, amid scuttling cockroaches and the detritus of rats, he sat on a moldy-smelling bed. Some previous guests had left a child's toy behind: a teddy bear. Involuntarily, Groznyy clutched it to him, cradling it as if it were a lost child suddenly returned. Now it was Groznyy's eyes that were vacant as he stared, terrified, into the gloomy room. He felt that the head of the teddy bear was wet. He imagined this must be blood from the fatal wound with which he had felled his son. Without thinking, he said aloud, "Absalom, my son." And again, "Absalom, my son."

As he nestled the teddy bear, he imagined he was caressing Modest's curls as fondly as he had done when Modest was an infant and which he should have continued to do when Modest was alive and cherishable: "My son, my dearest son, my life, my hope." The words resounded round and round but response came there none from the disappeared Modest. Groznyy's sins of omission flooded through his addled brain.

Suddenly, Groznyy was jolted out of his desperate reverie by an unmistakable smell coming from the toy. It was not wet with blood. It was damp with urine. This must have been why a family had left it behind, left it in this stinking hovel of a hotel, this vestibule to the hell that Groznyy had created for himself. He stared in the gloom. In his fevered imagination he waited, expecting some explanation. But there was nothing. No answer came. His

178

worst realization was that the void was in him. He was empty.

Two days after the fire, when Cesare Groznyy toured the ruins of Holy Cross Church, he saw how widespread the blaze had been. Aided by a strong gust of wind, it had turned into a short-lived tornado of destruction with six buildings consumed but, mercifully, only two people killed. The day after, sudden public anxiety and fear turned to disbelief. Not everything was gone on Milhous Avenue but it looked that way since, in addition to the rubble of buildings, gone also was all the regular street furniture of signposts and traffic points. The street itself looked like a bombed-out wasteland with heaps of charred debris punctuated by stubs of broken walls. The Groznyys' janitor neighbor who had helped Modest tend the wounded Arab man tried to stifle her tears as she told reporter Steve Sharp of the *Norse Hoven Courier*, "All those magnificent Milhous buildings that were the pride and joy of Norse Hoven and Babel City are now reduced to shapeless ruins."

Groznyy mouthed disbelief and shock but he was relieved. He knew well how to disguise his feelings because he understood that the fire would benefit him. He was jealous of the uninterested might of Milhous College and secretly rejoiced in the misfortune that covered his crime. All Groznyy cared about was that he had had a very narrow escape.

The police forensic team examined the remains of the two bodies in the remains of his house, Ashley's and Modest's, both seemingly burned out of recognition. In time, however, they were. Everyone assumed Modest had died from a mix of smoke inhalation followed by burning when he collapsed in a suffocating faint.

Groznyy did not want to face his wife's grief. At the table where they ate, Anna persisted in hiding her face in her hands. She still could not speak but he heard her silent reproaches loud and clear as if she was a skilled orator: "I don't want to look at you as long as I live."

He answered her unspoken reproach with, "This can't bring him back. What's done can't be undone."

Soon he understood that Modest dead was a far greater nuisance than he had been alive.

Both Modest's loves at second sight were united in misery so deep that they could not fathom it.

As she pieced together the public accounts of the disaster, Hermione sank into a depression of such listlessness that, when she moved, it was like someone in deep shock—which is what she was. Every time she tried to get some personal information about Modest she was thwarted. The phones in his home were down. Every extra detail reported on local radio and TV drew her inevitably to the horror of Modest's terrible death.

In her heart Hermione wanted to believe that Modest would have come back to her, must come back to her, once his infatuation with the deadly Lee-Holly had run its course. Now he belonged to neither of them, only to oblivion. Every time Hermione went over details in her mind, she cut herself off from thinking about Modest's death. Later, she could not have imagined she had so many tears inside her, welling up at any moment.

Holly's despair was just as deep. No tears would suffice. She had had lovers disappear before but they had never died—been killed by a mad incendiary, by a devastating fire.

Nothing mattered to Holly beside the personal loss of her beautiful lover. At first she did not care who had set fire to his house or what the impact of the fire would be on university politics. All she cared about was that it had shattered her life. For the first time in more years than she wanted to remember, she had opened herself up to unconditional love and she had had both her child and her lover destroyed in a week. Dr. Chicago prescribed sedatives. His tender care steadied Holly. Inwardly, she managed to steel herself for the ceremony of Modest's cremation that was delayed because of various police and state procedures since this had been arson and murder.

Out of charity, professors at BCU found a temporary home for the Groznyy family in the house of a colleague who was away in Europe on a sabbatical leave. The university health plan provided for temporary help, part maid, part carer for the ailing Mrs. Groznyy. Into this home in a manicured suburb, the interim maid let in the police. One was ambitious Italian American officer Lieutenant Leo Guerra. Groznyy noticed him casting a second look at the mixed-race maid with the translucent skin and then giving her a third glance.

By sheer force of will, when she shook the officers' hands in the hall, Anna put on a stoical attitude. They noticed that her face was ashen, making her dark eyes look like black holes in a corpse. But inside her she felt different. Primitive wailing seemed to be filling her head. Groznyy took the police officers into the sunroom, part gazebo, part porch, its glass windows replaced for summer by screens. Had the Groznyy family not been so troubled, this fairytale space with its plants and ferns somehow merging with the garden might have seemed idyllic.

Groznyy closed the door, but no matter how ill she was, Anna wanted to hear what was being said. She went out of the kitchen and cowered outside this summer bower, leaning on the side wall. At first she could hear nothing distinctly, only a sort of babble that made her predicament even more like an uncontrollable nightmare. Still shaky from what she knew was another bout of pneumonia, even if it was summer, her hands felt as cold as ice. Then the words from within the screens became clearer.

"We understand your distress but, before, the news leaks out, we have to tell you this."

Now Groznyy was shaken. Had they guessed his secret? Were they here to arrest him? The other man spoke.

"The blaze was terrible, even worse than if it had only been the result of arson by an unstable man mad with drink. The explosion was so bad because the fire triggered a bomb in your basement."

"A bomb? In the basement?"

"There's no doubt. Although the devastation was massive some artefacts—or parts of them—have survived. We can't be sure yet but the device may have been planted a short while ago. Wasn't there an incident—an Arab student found wounded by a small explosion from a drain outside your house? Do you remember?"

Groznyy's mind raced ahead. He was not thinking backwards to what was now a triple crime but forward to how this latest news would recast the murder. If the police had failed to see further when the little explosion had wounded the Arab man that Sunday morning, how would it look for them when the news about the bomb broke? Wouldn't their short-sightedness be taken as incompetence? Here was another cloak to cover his terrible crime.

The cops could tell that Groznyy was lost in his own reveries.

Leo Guerra spoke.

"Do you have any enemies?"

Groznyy did not answer directly.

"Who doesn't?"

"Yes, but enemies who would go to such lengths as placing an explosive device in your home?"

Groznyy knew how to deflect blame.

"Universities sometimes go through big changes—

academic shifts in policy. There are consequences for everyone who works there—professors and administrators alike. President Franklin Miler has been an inspirational, prophetic leader. But not everyone likes that. Change makes people uncomfortable. It can be threatening."

Groznyy thought the police wanted him to name names. But he knew better. Naming names, making accusations, would make the blame specific and might run the risk of counter charges. He would be safer if the cloud of terrorism remained foggy. He and Anna Stasinova must remain victims. People must see them as heroes. His eyes shifted. He did not want to show any sense of relief. That might give him away.

Outside, Anna was transfixed. She drifted off the half-heard words. Suddenly, she was gripped to a shiver. It was as if she was onstage with the villain when she heard one of the policeman say as clear as a bell, "Unfortunately, he was—I cannot put this delicately—burnt to a cinder: his limbs and bones, splinters—all mixed up, congealed. The fire fighters and forensic team needed a scalpel to separate the poor boy's legs from the collapsed beams."

The other policeman said, "But there's one thing. The pathologists could identify a blow to the right side of the head because of the way the skull, better preserved than the rest of him, was cracked."

No one was more skilled at omission than Cesare Groznyy. Prodded, he told the police how a collapse of beams must have been responsible for the blow to the head and that was why Modest had fallen prey to the flames.

"But that would not have been there on the right side of his face. It would have been on the left because of the position of the skull."

"But you said yourself that the havoc of the fire had jumbled everything—the house, poor dear Modest's body, everything."

"Then there's his ring."

"Ring?"

"Ring. It was a token from his ex-girlfriend, Hermione Eterna."

Groznyy blanched. "Damn him," he thought. "Two girl-friends. And I thought it came from the other one."

Leo Guerra suspected nothing. He continued.

"Apparently, he never took it off, even after they broke up."

Groznyy blanched again. This time he gulped. "But?"

"But we found it, not on Modest's body but trapped in a crack in a metal bracket on your bedroom floor. Can you suggest why it was there?"

Groznyy had to think quickly—recover his composure, put on his sad countenance again, and think damn quickly.

"Modest can go into our room. His mother keeps cleaning fluids there—liquids to clean her jewelry. Modest could use them whenever he wanted. He must have taken the ring off to clean it."

Outside, as she listened transfixed, once again came the accusing voice in Anna's head: she had raised dearest Modest for her loathsome husband to murder. His loss had sharpened the bitterness of her marriage. Her eyes, now too dry to cry, seemed to be blistering with fury. Anna slumped onto the ground. She was petrified. Her face was drawn so tight that it looked as if someone must be pulling the skin from behind for plastic surgery. Her eyes were staring so intensely they might have been about to pop out of her skull.

She fixed her eyes on paving stones cut into the grass. Transfixed, she felt she could somehow confide in them, pour out her sorrows, if only because they would not interrupt her. Compared with her husband's severity, their hardness seemed as pliant as candle wax. All Anna could think was that she never wanted to eat or drink again, not even to keep up her failing strength so she could be revenged on him.

She thought of Groznyy's other, absent child whom he paid for. She also thought about his first wife whom he had disposed of. Within her small frame, Anna felt her heart thump with outrage. She wanted to stifle its moans by drowning in her own tears—anything excessive so that the pain of living with this monster would come to an end. Then she looked hard at the stones again. The welcome heat of an early summer day gave off a gentle murmuring noise. It was, to her, like life departing from the world around her.

Groznyy's staff in the provost's office realized he was living in a terrible internal hell, psychological as well as political. Rumor was plentiful. Once, when Bee Flute was about to knock on his door, she heard him talking to himself.

"Who called me a murderer? Modest was killed in a fire, started by that mad arsonist."

When Bee told her husband, he said, "There are cynics everywhere. Well at least no one will say, 'The cause of the fire was the Insurance.'"

At Modest's funeral, when Cesare stood outside the chapel of the crematorium that held so many urns in its Garden of Rest, no matter how comforting its crosses, headstones, and urns, he felt himself persecuted by the residual energy of those who had passed away.

When it was his turn to speak, his words tumbled out easily enough.

"I've been provost for some time now. Whatever our political vicissitudes, I had hoped to find happiness in the bosom of my family. Now death, alas, has taken my son near the eve of his wedding. For all the unhappy tears that you see running down the wrinkles in my cheeks and those coursing down my wife's lovely face, please show pity for my dear son."

Anna was not moved. There they were: two middle-aged frauds divided by bitter secrets that, if exposed, would have torn apart the curtain of their marriage and ended Cesare's academic career forever.

While his silent wife was brimful with her own self-deluding reminiscences, Cesare was in his element. He could pronounce the obituary for his son as if by rote. Yet, as he continued his funeral oration, he felt his gray hair should be falling out with shame.

"Fate, cruel fate has condemned my beloved son to eternal rest earlier than it should. Though this second cremation must end the cruelty of the first, he is not dead, either to us or to the world. His ashes will stay here in these precious resting grounds to show he lives on in our hearts."

Ever the thieving magpie of insights from writers he disparaged, Groznyy took the theme of time, emphasizing its remorseless progress and analyzing its benign effects— notably its healing and restorative properties.

While he was speaking, he scanned the crowd to discern who had come from among the great and the good. He knew by sight not only his own faculty members but also leaders from other colleges, some of whom had come out of communal respect. Nevertheless, he was surprised to see Lucy Kaye, the officious dean of nursing at Norse Hoven University, a dumpy figure in black, hovering on the sidelines like a benign myna bird.

Lucy Kaye was known across NHU as the Commodore. No one could say if this was because she really was descended from the Vanderbilt family, or after her houseboat moored on Long Island Sound, or the saucy nautical expressions she used to keep her crew of shrill nurses in order.

When the ceremony was over and Groznyy was thanking

the mourners outside the chapel individually, he paid particular credit to her.

"Madam, I esteem you as an academic leader of proven integrity. You do us great honor. But I think you have more on your mind than our personal calamity."

"Mr. Provost, you are ahead of me. I grieve for you and your dear wife. You must forgive my interruption. But you are well aware that time and tide wait for none of us. We can find a political silver lining in this terrible tragedy. Terrible."

Groznyy had no idea what an ally this comparative stranger would prove to be.

For a minute he was distracted. He could see two other women on the edge of the mourners, both in black, one with a veil. One he recognized as the student pianist he had once heard play and whom Anna had told him Modest was dating. He liked her abundant Titian hair, her full figure shown off by her skimpy, student hand-me-down clothes. He dreaded recognizing the other woman. When she threw back her veil to kiss the student, it was her, the damnable singer who was now calling herself Holly Wood. A shiver of frustration shook him but it was momentary. Then he saw the two women move away together. He thought himself lucky they could not know anything. Damn their suspicions.

As she embraced Hermione cautiously, Holly said, "Forgive me. I knew he was with you but I fell in love with him just as you did. I hadn't the courage to say no when he asked me out."

Hermione was surprised but Benny had told her that something like this might happen. Besides, he had given her a script to follow.

"I don't think there is to be any wake. My boss, Benny Vincenzo, from the restaurant, sent me here in a car. We would be pleased to offer you a ride home, or wherever you're going, here in Norse Hoven, or Babel City, or Manhattan—that's where I'm heading."

"You're being kind," replied Holly, also surprised.

They walked past commemorative tablets embedded in a rippling curtain wall of stone at the side of the chapel. The wall was decorated with wilting flowers and some urns. The mix of Christian crucifixes—Catholic and Orthodox—and Egyptian stone symbols everywhere seemed unfeeling reminders both of the long dead and the recently departed. When the two women arrived at Benny's large car, Holly could not suppress a sigh of astonishment at another passenger already inside.

Groznyy could no longer see Modest's two girlfriends. He was drawn up sharp by Lucy Kaye's words in the chapel grounds.

"Through our schools of nursing and social work, education and theater, Norse Hoven University has long had a reputation as an academic pioneer among caring professions, starting in the 1930s when we were named Lazarus College."

Groznyy now had an inkling as to where this was leading. Lucy was surprised at how well informed he was.

"But, dearest lady, the downside is the way that NHU has bent academic disciplines as preparation for practical training so that, for example, biology is no longer the Discipline of Biology but a pre-med gateway for medicine at graduate school."

"Perhaps there's a grain of truth in that. Our success in placing students at med schools has certainly given the faculty the idea that they're as eminent as the most famous Ivy League professors, even though no one has ever published."

Lucy's snide putdown of her own professors found a ready audience in Groznyy.

"New faculty members are a rarity with us but older

faculty never lose their touch in turning them from teaching and research to university politics—us against them, professors against administrators. They indoctrinate them about the significance of labor unions."

"Dear lady, you are preaching to the converted. Older professors take the high moral ground of responsible radicalism with younger ones. However, their intentions are to bend the young professors, who want tenure and need their approval, to their own political interests."

"Exactly. This is where you come in."

Common conviction and common purpose wiped away their tears. As the princess looked hard at Hermione and Holly, she said, "If Groznyy is crime, we must not be revenge pure and simple, but moral retribution."

The three women sat with Benny in their widows' black weeds, although none was a widow. They were in his upstairs apartment above the Golden Cockerel, gazing intently at his toy theater presentation of the reception room in the provost's house on Milhous Avenue.

"It could not have happened the way the press say," argued Benny. "Modest was supposed to have been killed by smoke inhalation from the fire and the bomb explosion. But it could not have happened like that."

Benny adjusted the mechanism in the small room and lowered the ceiling beams as they might have collapsed in the fire. Lying atop the toy beams as they fell was a pigmy figure representing Modest.

"Why would Modest be found on top of the beam, not trapped underneath it if he was in the reception room when the fire started? And if he wasn't in the reception room but in the master bedroom, why was he there? And why, from a mangled door fragment that survived, was the key locking the bedroom door on the outside? Why would Modest have been locked in?"

"How do you know this?" asked Hermione.

"Dear Hermione," said the princess, "you know our clientele includes men in the FBI and the CIA. They tell him about crimes. We also know what Groznyy is capable of."

The princess cast a look at Holly that escaped Hermione but not Benny.

"We are the modern Euminides."

"What?" asked Holly.

The princess gave Holly a disdainful look. Benny intervened.

"Furies of vengeance. Hell hath no fury like a woman scorned."

The princess said, "We must expose the crime and nail the murderer. Holly, you have a good opportunity to scout out BCU. There's a fundraising concert next week. Go with Dr. Chicago. Sing there. Use your talents."

In case her double meaning escaped anyone, she added, "You must do whatever it takes."

Inside, Holly was terrified.

To signal her unspecified but firm intentions at the fundraiser concert at BCU, she forsook her little black dress for a blazing red sheath. It clung to her hourglass shape and set off her blonde hair. Holly knew she was there to find out anything she could. But inwardly she was too choked with conflicting emotions to think straight.

She would never have been able to make it down the corridor to the provost's office without Dr. Chicago by her side. She gripped his hand so tight that her nails drew blood. The blues-like lament that she thought she had heard on her last visit to BCU now seemed even more threatening. But Groznyy was all glacial smiles. He assumed his most seductive manner with flowery compliments to all artists in the concert. No one could guess that he had killed his son and his grandchild.

When it was Holly's turn to sing in the makeshift auditorium, it was a relief because she could avoid her tortured emotions and concentrate on what she did best. She imagined she was standing outside a grim and forbidding tower, Fortress Groznyy, inside which the soul of Modest lay imprisoned. It was torment. But Holly's love affair with Modest had opened a vein of refined sentiment in her art that had widened her range and softened her style. Now his death deepened her sense of tragedy and irony in the way she handled words and music. After the tragedy of Modest's death, she began voicing darker psychological undercurrents in her songs. When she sang "The Man That Got Away," it became more than the self-reproach of a woman who has loved and lost. For the man had been taken not by some lover's quarrel but by Death.

The audience grasped that there was some extra dimension to Holly's reflective singing. Because they did not know the personal details, they filled in the blanks of her elegiac interpretation themselves. Brad Gable sensed her serious undertones. They unsettled him. His unease deepened when Holly appropriated Che Guevara's number from *Evita*, "High Flying Adored," with its ironic questioning of a political icon. Holly was signaling to Groznyy that she was taking him on. If Holly was going to follow the princess's scenario of exposure and revenge, she decided it was going to be on her own terms.

Holly also imagined that new Arab eyes were following her every glance, her every inflection as a prelude to undressing her in their minds' eyes. A new Arab contingent assumed that Holly was trying to communicate something underhand—but what?

PRISONERS

First he got the phone call. He had returned from another US mission and found BCU in yet another crisis. Then the official letter arrived from Washington, D.C. Franklin Miller was to be appointed US ambassador to the Far East country of his dreams. It was to be the summit of his career. There would be clearance procedures but, soon, he would be up, up, and away. It would be a fond farewell to the university politics of Babel City University. Soon he could strut on the world stage of Pax Americana.

Suddenly, the pettiness of little BCU, the professors' interminable wrangles with Cesare Groznyy, their spitting insults like spiteful cherubim caterwauling in surround-sound, would evaporate. Miller already imagined himself knocking back cocktails on the plane carrying him to trysts with flashing almond eyes. He no longer cared what happened to Groznyy and his critics. He sat down to write his letter of resignation as president of BCU.

His conversation in the crematorium with the dean of nursing at NHU gave Groznyy the idea of reinventing himself—or, at least, his self-presentation. He would make a show of beginning a new era of governance. First, he made an emotional speech to professors and administrators. He asked for a united effort in the common cause of rebuilding the razed houses around Milhous Avenue.

"We have to address the consequences of the fire and its devastation. This has to be our priority. The energy survey in Science Park was invaluable for gathering information about labs and energy use. For that, we thank all the participants—the professors and the survey workers. But now we must concentrate on redevelopment of our physical plant."

Thus did Groznyy quench the tumult around the energy survey.

When he next met with Dean Lucy Kaye, it was ultra private in her office in NHU. Groznyy could assume seductive political charm. He kept his own counsel as he watched this petty head of nursing snivel her way round her desk. In her little kingdom, she barked out orders to her toads. It always surprised immigrant Groznyy how fond of titles like dean were these Republicans and Democrats of the oldest democracy in the world.

For her part, Dean Kaye saw in Groznyy a man of stern metal who could discipline the fractious professors, doctors, and nurses of NHU and BCU, and weld them into a cohesive team of academic excellence.

Lucy began simply: "You may have heard that our president, Caspar Corelli, has prostate cancer. It's terminal. He's going to retire at the end of the semester and spend his last months with his family."

Here was her offer. BCU and NHU should unite and pool all resources. Lucy would orchestrate a campaign for Groznyy's election as president of a newly conjoined BCU-NHU when Franklin Miller left—suppressing any evidence of failure—in exchange for her own promotion. She would be the new provost. In this way Groznyy would be able to snatch victory from the jaws of defeat with Lucy Kaye as his exultant provost.

Everything proceeded smoothly enough with Groznyy and Lucy counting on the immense sympathy within the academic community over the catastrophic fire and the tragic death of dear Modest, an up-and-coming artist cut down before his prime.

"They're so predictable," Groznyy said to Larry Dawdler as he described the trustees who directed the presidential search committee. "They're contemptible. They look like extinct animals. They have no more personality than a stuffed groundhog—old humanoid fiends with one foot in the grave, bleary eyes closed to new academic ideas."

Groznyy's diatribe hid his inner misgiving that some of these dotards might later stand up to him if he became president. Indeed, Groznyy was as two-faced as the old imperial Russian eagle. When the search committee interviewed him he brought his most flowery language to tempt them. He had skimmed the same Wagner libretto among his wife's LP sets as Modest had used to come clean to Hermione.

Groznyy knew tricks of rhetoric—intimate and grand. He made his voice deeper as he spoke to the search committee in order to demonstrate that the subject was important and so was the audience. He looked round the table fixing his eyes on everyone in turn so that they thought he was addressing them personally and would be flattered.

"I've come here, like spring in April, to free your minds from winter. Let's cut through the forest of complacency around NHU and BCU. Don't let the atrophied minds of your stale professors clog academic progress with envy and disappointment. You, the search committee, are better than that. Together, we—I as president, supported by your ambition—can sing a song of academic love."

The Commodore had never heard such romantic twaddle. She was not sure that it was appropriate but she was swept along by his words, nevertheless. However, she faced a new problem.

History secretary Claire Rollinsky was excited. She had heard it on the grapevine and could hardly wait to tell her boss, Mordred Stickleman. She wanted to use the new titbit to seal their sexual bond.

"Mordred, it's best you hear this from me. There's word across campus that, early in his career, Groznyy had some extramarital affairs, notably with someone named Esther Vashti with whom he had a love child."

Stickleman was ecstatic. Now he had Groznyy where he wanted him.

Anna's double pneumonia was getting worse. She was listless. In the past, her bouts of pneumonia had sapped her energy until she felt as threadbare as a limp leaf of lettuce. During her first bout of pneumonia years ago, Dr. Squires had told her she had abscesses in both lungs. Double pneumonia, Dr. Squires had said. Now the dull pain in her back from her infected lungs was sharper. When she stood up, it was just about bearable. But she did not have enough energy to stand for more than a few minutes. When she lay down, the pain increased so that she would toss and turn. And she still could not speak.

Groznyy was quick off the mark. Anna's illness put him in a quandary. If he called medical help, they would take Anna away to hospital. There she would, in all probability, break down. She might get her voice back and describe the murder of their son and the way Groznyy had forced her to keep quiet. When professors asked after Anna, Groznyy knew he could no longer delay calling Dr. Squires. But he also knew he could not leave the good doctor and Anna alone together. That might be fatal.

Dr. Squires was surprised by how considerate was Groznyy's new manner. Not the usual gruff, dismissive response of an uncaring spouse but the solicitous manner of a concerned husband. It was unusual for Groznyy to stay with the two of them while Dr. Squires examined Anna. He did not see the threatening looks Groznyy gave Anna over his shoulder.

Dr. Squires arranged for Anna to have an X-ray. At the clinic, Groznyy again acted the solicitous husband to perfection. The doctors gave Anna prescriptions for penicillin. She remembered them saying, "Amoxicillin." Groznyy made sure she took her pills regularly.

*

The former CIA man was back at BCU with another book to plug: *What the CIA Can Do for America*. He had been turned all right. Two months earlier, Franklin Miller had suggested casually to Mordred Stickleman that he invite the ever-presentable Todd Carter to speak to his older students. Now his message was going to be subversive and patriotic at the same time. And the title of his address was so unassuming: "A Little Talk."

After Stickleman introduced him grudgingly, they were off. Todd took off his tie and undid the top button of his button-down-collar shirt. He sat nonchalantly on the front desk and swung his legs as if he was a little boy. His manner was so inviting to these eager youngsters. He turned the little talk into a conversation so that the students thought they were in control.

"What do we know about terrorism and terrorists?"

Todd drew a worn, soft-cover Random House pocket dictionary from his jacket. He asked a student in the front row to read out the entry on terrorism: "The use of violence and threats to intimidate or coerce, especially for political purposes."

"What do you think, professor?"

"I think that's very tame, given the history of terrorism across the world," answered Stickleman.

Turning to the class, Todd asked, "Can you give some examples—suggest a few names?"

The class knew buzz words. Out tumbled a catalog of terrorists: "Anarchists," "the IRA," "ETA," "the Baader Meinhoff Gang," "the Red Brigade," "Carlos the Jackal."

"Any American examples?"

"The Haymarket Riot in Chicago, Wall Street bombs, Sacco and Vanzetti," said a girl with her hair in plaits.

"What do terrorists want?"

"They can't change society, get their own way politically, so they resort to acts of piracy or outrage," said the girl's bodybuilder boyfriend.

"Such as?"

"Taking hostages, hijacking planes, blowing up major buildings," continued the boy.

"Does any of this mayhem, these atrocities, ever lead anywhere?"

Stickleman wanted to show he was still in charge. He said, "Well, would-be revolutionaries used bombs to disrupt Russian society before World War I. Then, in the war, the Germans ferried the Bolsheviks into Russia by train to cause havoc and disrupt the Russian war effort against them. This led to the Bolshevik Revolution of 1917 that brought down the tsar."

Stickleman wanted to move the little talk forward. He asked, "Where do you see the future?"

"We are sitting on a time bomb. We face a new wave of terrorism. Terrorists before and during the twentieth century have been thugs, merciless destroyers of society and of people going about their regular lives—supporting their families and bringing up their kids—like all of you will do."

Despite himself, Stickleman admired Todd's skill that made everything he said accessible. Then Todd became more insistent.

"No matter how terrible terrorists were in the past, what lies ahead will be far worse. The roots of this new wave of terrorism can be traced to the mountainous area of Afghanistan. What do we know about Afghanistan?"

Todd had not expected an answer but he treated the silence as if the class had answered correctly.

"That's right. Afghanistan is a mountainous country in Central Asia. Political geographers tell me it's about the size of Texas. It's landlocked, which means—"

"No sea," said the girl with her hair in plaits.

"Right again. You're a good audience. Excellent. But you know that. Afghanistan borders Pakistan in the south and east, Iran in the west, some Russian states in the north, and China in the east. Anything else?"

An Italian American football scholar answered, "It's all mountains and desert—very hot in summer and very cold in winter."

"But what does Afghanistan have that people want?"

The clue was obvious. A voice from somewhere in the middle spoke up: "Mineral resources."

"I guess I'd have to get up very early in the morning to catch you out. What mineral resources? What would you guess?"

Others in the class wanted to join in. They named the usual suspects: "Coal," "iron," "copper," "gold," "uranium," "zinc," "natural gas," "petroleum."

"That's just a beginning. So, it won't surprise you that other countries are interested in Afghanistan."

By now the class was ready not only to listen but also to try and understand what Todd had to say.

"Sometimes, Afghanistan has had kings. Now it's a republic. And this is where we come in. In April 1978, the communist People's Democratic Party of Afghanistan—also known as the PDPA—seized power in the Sar Revolution. This new regime was dogged by controversy from the start. Why?"

A young woman with a Muslim headscarf said, "The PDPA declared equality of the sexes. They wanted to draw women into political life. This made conservatives angry."

"Well, you've done your homework. What happened next?"

"Uprising!" said a grad student wearing glasses that he kept adjusting.

"Uprising, that's right. Opponents of the PDPA started an uprising in eastern Afghanistan. The situation deteriorated into civil war with guerrilla forces—the mujahideen—against government forces across the country.

"What happened among Afghanistan's neighbors?"

Again, the clue was obvious.

"Other countries took sides with a vengeance," said the grad student.

"Yes. Nearby, Pakistan provided the Afghan rebels with covert training centers. Russia also got involved. On 26 December 1979 Soviet leader Leonid Brezhnev ordered a Russian invasion of Afghanistan."

"Inside Afghanistan there was also friction between different factions," said the Muslim girl. "Tens of thousands of young Muslims have traveled from all over the world to Afghanistan to fight the Russian invaders alongside the mujahideen. For them, this is a jihad—a holy war—against Russia."

"And behind the scenes?"

"One of the leaders is a man on a mission named Osama bin Laden, "continued the girl. "He's a Saudi multi-million-aire. His fortune comes from a family business in civil engineering. He uses his wealth to establish a network to locate, train, and supply Afghan fighters against the Russian invaders."

"Everything you've said is right. Excellent again. But this is also a war in a wider context: the Cold War between Russia and America. Although the Soviets claim they are only in Afghanistan to maintain order, their opponents in the West"—Todd pointed backwards to himself—"us—suspect them of other motives. Can you suggest what these might be?"

Again, out came the usual suspects. Students repeated lessons well learned.

"The Russkies want to use the situation in Afghanistan to move their borders southward into Pakistan and Iran," said the footballer.

Stickleman was now even more suspicious of Franklin Miller's seemingly helpful offer—presenting his students with this WASP guy who made information accessible.

Mordred realized that Miller was also testing Todd, auditioning him. He also suspected that he, too, was being monitored. He found himself increasingly jealous of Todd for his facile charm and his ability to put everyone at ease.

"Well what are we to do about it?" continued Todd. "It's not simply a matter of imperial greed or the relentless hunt for oil among the big powers. There is a deep human tragedy here. The Russian invasion has caused the deaths of over a million Afghans, mostly civilians."

Then came the *coup de grace*. Todd asked, "Why are we interested?"

Without any hesitation, up rose a common cry from the class: "To stop the spread of communism!"

Todd carried on.

"What was the United States to do? We didn't want Russia in Afghanistan. Rather than have US soldiers in Afghanistan in a war that has also involved the UK, the western allies have chosen to fight indirectly, using proxies to do their fighting for them. That is their strategy. So they have trained these fighters. The mujahideen have been training secretly in the UK."

Todd referred to a paper on the desk beside him. He held it up.

"The British Special Air Services—the SAS—provide weapons training. They have trained Afghan rebels in Scotland at secret camps—as agreed to by the British prime minister, Mrs. Thatcher. She's supposed to have said of our esteemed president, 'Poor dear, there's nothing between his ears,' but when he clicks his fingers she comes to heel like a bitch on command. She toddles over.

"The US has allowed the mujahideen to buy American weapons at rock bottom prices. The CIA and the British SAS have cooperated with one another. The mujahideen wanted this. Osama bin Laden—that's the guy with the money— once posed for photos with a Stinger machine gun.

"What happens if and when the USSR leaves Afghanistan? What happens to these soldiers, all armed and trained? And what happens to their weapons?"

The class was all ears.

"Your professor asked about future danger. Here's the thing.

"We have armed our enemies. Despite the help we have given them, they loathe us with undying passion. They hate our commercial penetration of the world. They hate our support of Israel. They want to destroy us. And we have given them the means. They are mostly young. Their energy and commitment are inexhaustible. Yes, you might say that these so-called Afghan Arabs have been pawns. They've been encouraged, equipped, trained and supplied by America, Britain, and also the Arab states of the Gulf.

"Don't underestimate them. These militants are not a rag-tag army of incompetents. They are ready for the next millennium, skilled in modern methods of death. They are tigers at the gates.

"An open society has its enemies. Society needs its guardians, its safe-keepers, its CIA, to exercise eternal vigilance. The CIA will dig deep to find out and uncover what we all need to know but are afraid to ask."

Stickleman was silenced. This was not what he wanted to hear. It was, however, what the young Rambos in the class did want to hear. Now they wanted to join the CIA.

"Mission accomplished," said Franklin Miller when he heard how the little talk had gone.

But Miller did not know about the two epilogues to the little talk.

In the courtyard outside the shabby lecture room a mini demonstration of young people was jostling the audience as they left. Some protesters were students wearing clothes in the default costume of western students—T-shirts, blouson jackets, artistically scruffy jeans, and sneakers. Others wore exotic costumes from different Middle Eastern countries with differences too subtle for Todd to distinguish. Many bore placards with aggressive slogans in support of Palestine:

"Death to Western Capitalist Pigs!" "Root out Jewish Finances from Washington!" "Free the Palestinian People!" "Eliminate Israel!"

Todd slipped through them and into a downtown diner for over-easy eggs and French fries. An unknown burly man sidled into the chair opposite him. It was Mukhtar who came straight to the point.

"I enjoyed your talk more than I can say. I'm one of your tigers at the gates. You're right. The US has taught us well. You have your multinational companies, like ITT and the Seven Sisters—capitalist corporate giants whose international coils elude national governments. They have gleaming offices around the world but they use modern technology to move their physical headquarters when the going gets tough. They move from country to country, city to city, with just a flick of a switch. And we can do just the same."

Todd was too experienced an operative to respond to the latent threat behind Mukhtar's insistent smile.

"And then there's your popular culture of action movies with all-American muscled superheroes responding to ultra-smooth villains with bombs and gunfire, winning their private wars by shooting from the hip and asking questions later. There's a direct line from macho Wild West shootouts to the latest Hollywood gung-ho blockbuster. Your culture celebrates destruction. Don't think we haven't learnt from you. We're ready to give you fire for fire."

There was an outsize blare from a police car outside. Todd looked through the diner windows. When he looked back Mukhtar was gone.

Not in a shabby lecture room somewhere in America but in Afghanistan, would-be terrorist Ramzi Yousef did not know if he was in a tunnel or a pit. Todd did not mention Yousef in his little talk for Yousef was still unknown. Yet he was living the life of the sort of young Muslim radicals Todd had been describing.

Terrorist Ramzi Yousef was as dangerous an explosive as any bomb he was learning to concoct, and far more lethal. Yousef had turned his education at the expense of western society into the most dangerous cunning and ruthlessness. He knew how to store up his hatred as surely as he would store his hard-won knowledge and hard-earned lethal chemicals. He knew how to hide in open view, how to fight and evade capture, or be ready to die.

In the psychological pit below Yousef were his confused memories of his mixed origins, part Palestinian, part Saudi, and memories of his parents who had lived in different places in Pakistan and Saudi Arabia. And his overactive mind was always speaking to him as if to camera.

"In dry and barren Baluchistan in southwest Pakistan I've seen extreme poverty with people spending winter in wooden huts and summer in threadbare tents. When my father, Karim, settled us in Turbat, a Baluchistan town of a hundred thousand people, we found ourselves at a bizarre crossroads with shops selling 300 types of dates aside heroin—a tantalizing product for western decadents."

In the psychological tunnel behind Yousef lay his education. He had moved in and out of the UK, spending time in Oxford as a language student and in Wales at Swansea, studying engineering while he honed his appreciable skills in applied chemistry.

"I was a hyperactive fool. Like many young guys let off the leash of home restraints, once I was in a college in the West, I wanted—and got—sex and drugs and rock 'n' roll just like everyone else. But I have no regrets about the years when I strayed. This strengthened my reawakening to the true religion and my moral conviction. I found religion and my great purpose psychologically liberating. That wouldn't have happened had I not sowed my wild oats."

Indeed. In Afghanistan where he went to fight in 1988, Yousef found he was among over 25,000 young foreign jihads from, maybe, thirty-five countries. Yousef, like many, sought the thrill of adventure as well as a sense of purpose.

He had already learned deep hatred of Israel and what he saw as Israel and its allies' harsh treatment of the Palestinian people. This hatred nestled alongside his comfortable hatred of western consumer society.

Cesare Groznyy and many another American megalomaniac CEO may have thought they were electrifyingly dangerous. But Ramzi Yousef left them at the starting post. Yousef wanted to detonate the entire capitalist West by blowing up its cherished icons, pulverizing the infrastructure, the commerce, and innumerable lives within its most famous city, New York. His commitment to the cause of the Palestinian people meant the destruction of everything else. His belief in his duty and his arrogant self-importance had obliterated any sense of perspective.

At BCU they had their illusions and their mind games.

The Groznyy Gang believed in unquestioning loyalty to Cesare Groznyy—whatever the personal cost to them. Groznyy believed he had an immortal destiny as a great academic leader. He was on a mission to root out and destroy his enemies while amassing a not-so-secret fortune.

His enemies in the Opposition Party liked to think they were idealists and skilled communicators. All they had to do was to destroy the little red devil in their midst who had come unwanted with his grandiose, empty promises and was determined to shuffle the pack of academic cards to their disadvantage.

Then there was the unofficial subversive Oryx Party. Its priority was to rid Palestine and Afghanistan of western capitalist interests, to eliminate the great scourge of Israel, to jolt the United States out of its detestable complacency by shaking the very foundation of Corporate America. Like the Groznyy Gang and the Opposition Party, these supposed zealots also believed they were movers and shakers. But not yet. It was a case of Paradise Postponed.

Each of these three university groups was not only defined by its illusions, but also confined by them. They wanted power. Inwardly, they were terrified of a future they could not predict. Power was to prove an elusive commodity. It was as if power did not want them.

Without the pressure of an agitated meeting with their young Arab stallions straining at the leash, the dean of psychology and the chair of chemistry could think about university politics in the universities more calmly. They saw how they mirrored macro global politics.

"You're right," said Ace Ferrari over dinner. "The Cold War will come to an end. We don't know when but we can guess why: the arms build-up with Reagan spending more money than Brezhnev. The West will bore at the innards of the East until it bursts Soviet repression. When the end comes, we will be there. Then we will strike."

"It's true, I tell you," Mordred Stickleman told Steve Sharp, investigative journalist for the *Norse Hoven Courier*. "This Esther Vashti is well over ten years younger than Groznyy. About five years ago, she began pressing Groznyy to leave Anna Stasinova. When he refused, she moved to the state with her child, ready to pounce. Now Groznyy is a candidate for president of BCU, she's threatening to go public about their tawdry affair. It's obviously true. Groznyy hasn't disclosed the relationship to the universities. No. But the proof is in a cache of secret Groznyy love letters."

"Yes," said Steve Sharp, determined not to give too much away. "I've heard the story. But so far, it's only rumor."

Thus prodded, and while realizing that Stickleman's interest was far from impartial, author Sharp started to dig for dirt, calling in a few journalistic favors, planning a kiss-and-tell article, "The Shame of BCU." Then he had a break. He took a call from lawyer Boris Goodenough and met him in a diner in downtown Norse Hoven.

"I'll come clean. Yes, my sis was in love with Groznyy. She was just a kid. He used her. But he couldn't discard her when it suited him. We saw to that. Yes, she kept his love letters—pretty trashy they are, too, believe me. My mom kept them in a shoe box at the bottom of a broom closet."

"Any chance?" started Steve Sharp.

"Sure, I thought you would ask," replied Boris Goodenough.

He opened his briefcase.

"Here are two. They're photocopies, of course. I've moved the originals to a bank vault."

Unlike Stickleman, Steve had no prurient interest in other people's sex lives. But he was interested in the power play at BCU and how it would pan out. Now he had seen some of the tawdry correspondence, it seemed here was proof that Groznyy had, indeed, enjoyed an off-on relationship with Esther Vashti. That was the story but Steve could not get any more details.

When Groznyy's own lawyer, Larry Dawdler, heard that Stickleman was agitating against Groznyy, he said, "Chief, you've got to get rid. Sock it to him."

And things did not go according to Stickleman's scenario. Once the search committee for president learned of the Groznyy-Vashti affair, it was too late for them to find someone else without risking public ridicule. Dean Lucy Kaye, who had staked her all on getting Groznyy elected so that she could become provost, moved heaven and earth to buy off Esther Vashti. To stop the scandal breaking, she got Dawdler to persuade the anonymous Texan donor for a projected theater renovation at BCU to send Esther and her child abroad. The donor was supposed to have paid her over $100,000 to keep quiet. Thus she became that rarity, a shady lady who successfully extorted money from a university, albeit most minor.

So skilled was Groznyy that Anna's illness played into his shabby campaign to become president of the soon-to-be conjoined universities. Lawyer Dawdler moved fast. At his request the letters Groznyy wrote to Esther Vashti were confiscated. People said that Dawdler was acting on behalf of Groznyy's betrayed wife, Anna Stasinova. Everyone knew she was desperately ill and everyone sympathized with her. Because of the embargo on the Vashti love letters, Steve's projected article collapsed.

Nothing now stood in the way of Groznyy's election. Given the machinations of the presidential campaign, if any sweetener was necessary for Lucy, it was that the new provost would take over the retiring president's house since the retiring provost's house was in ruins. And the new president himself would have a new house overlooking Long Island Sound to be built by Veronica Veneer's construction company. The new president of the augmented Babel City University glanced at his reflection in the hall mirror. He was transfixed. What he saw was an image of the prisoner of Babel City University. And the prisoner in the mirror looking back out at him realized there was no escape.

In her temporary home, pneumonia on top of her severe emotional distress made Anna more abject than ever. It was as if her body was shutting down, leaving her imprisoned in her mind. Over and over, she recalled the murder, how Modest had fallen; how Groznyy had dragged his body out of sight; and how, with a vice-like grip, he had pulled her downstairs after him. Trapped and exhausted though she was by her illness, her hatred of her husband, and her overwhelming grief, Anna knew she must do something.

She wondered if she could dress herself, get a taxi to the railroad station, get the train to New York, and then on to the restaurant where she felt sure Benny Vincenzo, Modest's friend, would help her get to safety.

When Anna tried to rise out of bed, she tottered and fell back. She passed out. When she came to and looked at the bedside clock, it was three hours later. She rose again with more determination. This time she got as far as to put her clothes on. She knew she must look like some bag lady in charity clothes. Could she make it to the door? Would it kill her?

Mordred Stickleman could not believe it. Not only had Cesare Groznyy somehow pulled victory from the jaws of defeat but he had also emerged fortified by the contest. He was not simply the discredited provost of little BCU who would never find work at a university anywhere again. Instead, he was the charismatic leader of an augmented university forged by the annexation of NHU by BCU. He would be strengthened even more as manager of a science park and a hospital complex that drew international prestige from Milhous College.

"Damn him to blazes!" said Mordred Stickleman to his wife. "He thinks he's electrifying. He relishes every twist and turn in his double-dealing journey to power. Damn him to hell."

The phone rang to interrupt this tirade at the dinner table.

"It's Claire," said Pauline sweetly when she answered it.

Before Mordred could get angry Claire said, "I know you don't want me to call you at home but you must hear this. Now Anna's gone, Groznyy has asked Holly Wood to marry him. She's accepted. It's all over campus."

As the handset fell, it was clear to Pauline that envy and

fury had gripped Mordred. It was as if they were boring into his innards. He felt his bones must be turning to marrow and pulp. He was beside himself.

"Shall I see Groznyy triumph? I would rather go into the abyss of disgrace he deserves. Let tigers tear me apart if I don't bring him down."

"Yes, dear," said Pauline. "But is that really necessary? I hear he causes so much trouble wherever he goes, makes so many mistakes, that he's determined to fail. They say he's his own worst enemy."

"Not while I'm still alive."

The story continues in
War in Pieces 2:
The Holly Wood Years of Ivan the Terrible

AFTERWORD and ACKNOWLEDGEMENTS

Why not? If we can have a *Lady Macbeth of Mtsensk* and a [King] *Lear of the Steppes* can we not have a modern *Ivan the Terrible*? *Lady Macbeth of Mtsensk* reworks the tragedy of a mesmerizing anti-heroine, first by Nikolai Leskov in his novel and then by Dimitri Shostakovich in his uncompromising opera based on that novel. William Shakespeare's original Lady Macbeth is, unlike Ivan the Terrible, a fictional character. But in eleventh-century Scottish history as Gruoch, queen to Macbeth, she was a real person. And the historical Ivan IV became fictitious as successive regimes in Russia re-presented his past achievements to support their own present policies, sometimes in ways more macabre than the original.

If you have ever endured a megalomaniac boss, chances are you have made unfavorable comparisons between him and dictators of the 1930s. You might also have noticed his hatred and fear of minorities, whether social, religious, or economic. A comparison with Ivan the Terrible of Russia might be more apt than Hitler or Mussolini for the late twentieth century—a period when we could lose count of the number of megalomaniac dictators across the world.

What about those aspects of Ivan's career and life for which he is widely known? His eight serial marriages equal to many a Hollywood star? His killing his son and heir-- familiar fodder on TV crime shows? His intimidating others like a gangster in film noir? His coteries of toadies as in Mafia and Soviet legends? His narcissistic character disorder?

Isn't this familiar in the corporate and political worlds as well as in TV soap operas?

As to threats from the East that confronted Ivan, well, threats from the East remain a profound problem for modern governments.

Cesare Groznyy, antihero in this *War in Pieces* novel, presumes to take on the might of Ivan IV. Hence Ivan's story is reconfigured making him president of an American university and emblematic of how leaders in West and East did business in the Cold War. Purely American details come from the corrupt presidency of Warren Harding and the Ohio Gang as unfolded by Mark Sullivan in *Our Times: The Twenties*.

Whereas the original Ivan faced up to challenges from the East and in so doing helped define Russian identity, our modern Ivan, like many a political leader in the 1990s, does not face up to terrorist fanatics who burst on the scene with the first bomb on the World Trade Center in 1993. Their leader, Ramzi Yousef, was a misfit fanatic, vitriolic in his condemnation of Israel and his unfocused support of the Palestinian people. Ramzi Yousef is a real and historical character but he is also, as the lead song of a musical has it, his own special creation, taking on and discarding other names. His public words and actions were first and most famously described from written and oral sources in journalist Simon Reeve's pioneer bestseller, *The New Jackals*. Since that groundbreaking exposure of the early days of Al Qaeda, there has been a wealth of information on the Internet, much culled from newspapers and sources in the public domain. I have drawn from some of these as well as Simon Reeve's work. But what I imagine might be Ramzi Yousef's private thoughts are here in my own words.

The Oryx Party, a secretive group at Babel City University, part supplier of relief for Palestinians, part cheerleader for Hamas, part cadre of angry Afghan Arabs, is my invention, my representation, of what may have been 200 or 300 such groups across the US in the 1990s. There was plenty of testimony in the late 1980s and 1990s of the resentment of angry young men from the Middle East at the West's way of doing business and their unfocused hatred of what some critics later termed the Anglosphere. The most devastating product of this hatred came with flying airplanes into the World Trade Center on September 11, 2001, causing the demolition of the Twin Towers and horrible loss of life.

Whatever the outcome of the war on terror, we can be sure that Hollywood, most famous center of movie making and symbol of showbusiness around the world, will survive both economically and psychologically. In this novel the epitome of its charm and enticement is the rising singer who takes the showbiz name of Holly Wood and, like Hollywood itself, being an ultimate survivor, takes on Cesare Groznyy and his son, Modest.

The 1993 bomb attack on the World Trade Center was not immediately seen as a decisive turning point in world affairs. I was in New York the day of the attack. My words here come from what I knew at the time, learnt later, and read about in various accounts that followed over the next twenty years.

Surely, a university or two can serve as an emblem of society just as well as the mighty Mississippi River or a Broadway chorus line. Among influences on this book was the notorious case in New York wherein the State Board of Regents investigated the trustees of Adelphi University and dismissed all but one of them in 1997. The *New York Times* covered the case with first-hand observations, interviews, and court records in articles, many by Bruce Lambert, whose account of the shenanigans makes diverting reading. The Regents' hearings took place while the cases against Ramzi Yousef neared their climax.

As to using personal experience, Modest's sensory impairment described in the book comes from my umbrella eye condition that moves between limited sight, partial sight, and legal blindness. However, apart from the ever self-inventive Ramzi Yousef, the characters in this novel are fictions, based on impressions and observations of various people. These fictional composites do not represent specific individuals alive or dead.

Full of quotations, whether mischievous or straight-faced, this novel certainly is. Many works of art, music, and literature are referenced in the text. Works referred to but not specifically acknowledged in the text include four Russian operas: Rimsky-Korsakov's *The Tsar's Bride* and *The Golden Cockerel*, Mussorgsky's *Boris Godunov* (as well as the Trepak from his *Songs and Dances of Death*); Shostakovich's *Lady Macbeth*, aka *Katerina Ismailova*; also, Bartok's *Bluebeard's Castle*.

I have also drawn from ideas in classic literature: in Shakespeare's *Titus Andronicus*; and the *Tales of a Thousand and One Nights*; and in modern literature from Ken Follett's *The Man from St. Petersburg*.

Two friends read the manuscript and offered constructive suggestions from different perspectives. I thank Kenneth McArthur and Andrew Donnelly. Their sharp responses helped strengthen the book.

I also thank Miles Bailey, director of the Choir Press, his colleagues Rachel Woodman and Adrian Sysum, and the copy-editor Fiona Thornton for their care, diligence, and courtesy in preparing the book for publication.

Sean Dennis Cashman,
Manchester 2015.

ABOUT THE AUTHOR

After studies at Oxford and Yale, Sean Dennis Cashman combined careers as a professor of American history and a writer, principally for New York University Press and the Ford Foundation, and as a music and theater journalist in New Haven, Connecticut. His classic history for NYU Press, *America in the Gilded Age*, has remained a focal text on the period 1865–1901 since it was first published in 1984.

In *War in Pieces*, he draws on his wide experience at eight universities to bring varied characters and a compelling story to engrossing life as he suggests terrible dilemmas facing modern western democracies when the era of the Cold War passed into an Age of Terror. His other books include:

Luke Reader, Blind Detective, 2012

America Ascendant: From Theodore Roosevelt to FDR in the Century of American Power, 1901–1945, 1998

America in the Gilded Age: From the Death of Lincoln to the Rise of Theodore Roosevelt, 1984,1988, 1993

America in the Twenties and Thirties: The Olympian Age of Franklin Delano Roosevelt, 1989

America in the Age of the Titans: The Progressive Era and World War I, 1988

SEAN DENNIS CASHMAN

CASHMAN

Luke Reader

blind detective

AMERICA
ASCENDANT

From Theodore Roosevelt to FDR
in the Century of American Power, 1901-1945

SEAN DENNIS CASHMAN

SEAN DENNIS CASHMAN

AMERICA

FROM THE DEATH OF LINCOLN TO

IN THE

THE RISE OF THEODORE ROOSEVELT

GILDED

THIRD EDITION

AGE

Lightning Source UK Ltd.
Milton Keynes UK
UKOW02f1623270416

273096UK00001B/63/P